# Bitch Lit

Edited by
**Maya Chowdhry** & **Mary Sharratt**

First published in 2006 by Crocus
Crocus books are published by Commonword Ltd,
6 Mount Street, Manchester M2 5NS

These stories are works of fiction and any resemblance
to persons living or dead, or to companies or authorities
is purely coincidental

Crocus books are distributed by Turnaround Publisher
Services Ltd, Unit 3, Olympia Trading Estate, Coburg
Road, Wood Green, London N22 6TZ

Cover design: bonnie and clyde
steph@bonnieandclyde.biz

Printed by LPPS Ltd
www.lppsltd.co.uk

British Library Cataloguing-in-Publication Data: a
catalogue record for this book is available from the
British Library

# Contents

# Interview with the Editors

*So what is Bitch Lit?*

**Mary Sharratt**: Bitch Lit is a smart and subversive celebration of female anti-heroes: women who take the law into their own hands, who defy society's expectations, who put their own needs first and don't feel guilty or get exterminated as a result!

**Maya Chowdhry**: Above all it's about women who refuse to be victims.

*Why focus on Women anti-heroes?*

**MS**: Bad girls aren't celebrated in art or popular culture the same way that men are. Literature is full of loveable male rogues, whereas transgressing women are depicted as witches. As a society, we condone men behaving badly – we continue to idolise the James Deans, George Bests, Liam Gallaghers and Pete Dohertys of this world. High-profile women on the other hand are all too quickly vilified by the media the moment they display any signs of zealous ambition or louche behaviour.

**MC**: I think women have generally been more censored in their writing than men and it's time we changed that. Male writers don't seem to have a problem creating anti-heroes – there's plenty of Dick Lit out there already!

### Is Bitch Lit a new genre?

**MC**: It's not a term you'll find in the dictionary – yet! Of course, writers were creating stories about strong female characters before we came up with the idea of Bitch Lit, just in the same way that there were lots of books written about simpering women before someone in a marketing department coined the phrase Chick Lit.

**MS**: There are some great examples of women anti-heroes in literature and popular culture (Medea, Lady Macbeth, Madame Bovary, Thackeray's Becky Sharp, and Thelma and Louise, for example) but most of them feature in cautionary tales where the wicked woman ultimately gets her come-uppance. More recently we've seen the hugely successful publication of Lionel Shriver's *We Need to Talk About Kevin* and Zoe Heller's *Notes on a Scandal*, demonstrating that there is a hunger for literature exploring the darker side of the female psyche.

### Did you have a good response to your call for Bitch Lit?

**MS**: I was amazed by the wealth of stories we received. About a decade ago, *Hurricane Alice*, a feminist literary journal in the US, solicited stories on the theme 'Legends of Bad Women'. However, when the themed issue was published, the editors lamented the dearth of stories about women who were really, seriously *bad*. Most of the fiction concerned women who were slightly grumpy, or more assertive than expected, or who were really victims lashing out in self-defence. It appeared that 'Bad Women' who live up to the name were a taboo subject, even among self-identified feminists. I was worried we might have a similar response. Thanks to Arts Council funding, Maya and I had the distinct advantage of being able to go out into the community and offer free workshops to help inspire and generate the kind of stories we were looking for.

### Are you being purposefully provocative in using the 'B' word?

**MC**: Artists and their work should be challenging. The word *bitch* obviously has a lot of negative connotations – but what we're doing is encouraging people to unpack the word – to think about how the word has been used as a way of silencing strong-minded women and disarming it through appropriation – in the same way that *nigger*, *paki*, *queer* and *dyke* have been reclaimed in some instances.

**MS**: In North America, publications such as *Bitch* magazine and the *Stitch 'n Bitch* guide to knitting have made the B-word increasingly acceptable, if still edgy and subversive. Many English people, on the other hand, have a true horror of the B-word. Some workshop participants appeared very timid and unsure about this whole Bitch thing, but once we discussed the true nature of Bitch Lit and started the exercises, something amazing happened. They got stuck in, embraced their inner Diva and Bunny Boiler, and wrote gleeful tales of barbecuing the neighbour's dog, stealing the boss's Viagra, sabotaging their ex and so on.

### *What can we expect to find in Bitch Lit?*

**MC**: A range of styles and genre: horror to humour and Bitch Romance to Bitch Mystery are used in surprising ways to bring us poetic meditations, psychological drama and literary playfulness.

**MS**: They range in tone from the light-hearted *A Fairy's Story* to the savagely funny *Pancake* and *Reader, I Mullered Him* to dark, disturbing tales of wrath and revenge, such as *Big Bad Momma* and *Lambswool*. All of these stories, in one way or another, are about women and power. They are the opposite of cautionary tales. They goad us and dare us to strip off our niceness, be real, leave our safe haven and go out into the dark woods knowing that the most dangerously sublime thing to be encountered in that forest is ourselves unleashed.

# LOUISE WILFORD
## Pancake

You can tell a lot about a man from the way he rolls a pancake in a Chinese restaurant. My first husband used to overfill his, so their edges strained to meet, like the waistcoat stretched taut across his beer belly.

Greed.

Though he did leave me rich when he died, so he wasn't all bad.

Brian rolls his pancakes up too loosely so lumps of duck, shredded spring onion and cucumber batons fall out of the end when he takes a bite, like weed from a badly rolled spliff. He's doing it now, blotting hoi sin off his silk tie with his napkin and giving an apologetic shrug. No grace. No dexterity. Money can't buy you style.

I must say, *Jake* is doing very well. Ten out of ten. He drips the sauce on expertly, spreading it round his pancake with the back of his spoon in a series of sensuous circles, catching my eye. Just the right amount of duck too. He chooses the best pieces, those with succulent flesh and just a touch of wrinkled, crispy skin, but doesn't take too many of them. He leaves some for us.

He has confident, experienced fingers.

He's turned out to be quite different from what I imagined when Angie first invited us out to meet her new boyfriend.

'Yes, I'd love one. Thank you,' I say.

The tips of his long brown fingers brush against mine as he passes me the pancakes. His nails are pale and square, neatly filed; students don't seem to have calluses on their writing fingers these days like they did when I was young.

'So, Jake,' I say, 'how are you finding the university?'

He starts telling me about his MSc course, with Angie – she's Brian's niece – butting in at regular intervals like a metronome. He looks me straight in the eye throughout the conversation, rarely turning towards his girlfriend though she is peering up at him with the adoring devotion of a cretinous Labrador.

She's straightened her hair and put in thick streaks the colour of Lucozade. It's a problem with owning your own beauty salon: since Brian set her up in that little business, she's been treating herself like a guinea-pig for every new beauty product that comes along. Her problem is she doesn't know what suits her. I've tried to drop hints, but she just seems too dense to notice. It's like flagging down a minicab in a thick fog.

*Self-knowledge* is what's needed. Take me, for instance. I've dyed out a few grey hairs and I had that gap in my teeth sorted years ago, but I'd never consider Botox. And *I* know what suits me. This dress, for instance: it cost a fortune and there aren't many women my age who can wear red.

Jake likes it. I can tell.

But what on earth does he see in *her*?

The salon *is* doing rather well, however.

Brian is busy juggling with a split pancake that's leaking hoi sin sauce all over the plate. A cucumber breach is imminent. There it goes, bits of sticky salad dropping into his lap. Angie passes him her napkin, an expression of fond concern on her wasp-sting face. Jake turns his head briefly, momentary polite interest widening his eyes, then turns back to me, giving me that lacerating, challenging look he used earlier when we first met. I can see he fancies me. You don't get to my age without being able to pick up on these things.

He's asking me whether I have a computer.

'Yes, of course,' I reply. 'But I can't seem to get it to work properly.'

Brian, slurping his Merlot, launches into a diatribe against Microsoft; he's the director of a chain of computer superstores so I suppose he's entitled to an opinion, but I've heard his opinions so often since we married that, frankly, he bores the pants off me. As he talks, he dips his sticky fingers into a dish of spiced cashew nuts the waiters brought to our table as an appetiser when we arrived (they've only started doing this since Jamie Oliver told the papers The Dancing Lion was his favourite Chinese restaurant, which made it into something of a celebrity-magnet and put Bath on the map – you used to be lucky to get prawn crackers). The nuts are flying everywhere, but Brian doesn't notice. Honestly, you'd think a man in his position would have learned a little finesse.

Jake listens patiently, however, occasionally murmuring something politely sympathetic, but he glances at me now and then with an unmistakeable twinkle in his eye that Brian is too full of Merlot to notice – though I suspect Angie has seen it. She throws me a perplexed and slightly hurt look, as if I *care* what Brian's silly little beautician niece thinks! I ignore her, looking steadily at Jake with what I calculate to be an expression of controlled interest – a hint, I hope, of hidden impulses beneath the surface etiquette.

I slip my foot out of my Jimmy Choo strappy sandal and press my toes gently against his shin through the cream linen of his trousers.

'Maybe Jake wouldn't mind coming over to take a look at our machine,' I suggest. 'I'm at home most afternoons.'

Jake blushes. Yes, really. A pink glow steals up his neck and his hand involuntarily moves to the spot before he rubs his ear as if he's got a cashew nut lodged in there. It's the first uncertain movement he's made all evening. I hold his gaze and he looks down, straightening his napkin. My toes move stealthily up his leg to his inner thigh. He takes a deep breath; his hand drops to his lap then down beneath the table-cloth to rest for a moment on the arch of my foot. I can feel the warmth of his fingers through the sheer mesh of my stockings. I wriggle my toes, looking all the while at Brian as if I'm concerned about whether or not he's enjoying his starter.

Angie is explaining that Jake is a computer programmer, not a handyman, and she gives me a brief, poisonous glance – which I ignore – and then Nigel, the gay Chinese head waiter who absolutely adores me, is at our table asking if we're ready for the soup course. Brian scowls slightly and nods – he's never liked Nigel since he took to calling him 'young man' in an ironical tone of voice.

Nigel stands behind Jake, squeezing his shoulders in an over-intimate way and waggling his eyebrows at me suggestively. He asks if we'd like any *sauce* with our main course, and winks. Brian is too busy trying to get bits of cashew nut out of his fingernails with a hot flannel to notice this little pantomime, thank God.

'Just the soup for the moment, please, Nigel,' I say, with a warning edge to my voice.

He gets the message and flounces away to the kitchen, stopping off at various tables *en route* to ingratiate himself with the evening's trawl of B-list celebs.

My foot is back in my shoe by now and I'm just

wondering what havoc Brian will cause with his wan tons, when Angie suddenly squeals like a piglet and begins pointing, apparently at Brian's head. Turning in my seat, I spot the huge spider which is running up the wall behind us and is about to embark on an expedition across one of the rather tacky black and white paintings of crabs and lotus-blossom with which the restaurant is adorned.

Angie, looking like a startled squirrel, pushes back her chair with a loud scraping noise and leaps to her feet, her glass tipping over and dousing Jake's trousers in red wine. He staggers to his feet and she clings to his arm, doing her 'helpless little girl' routine, but he's too furious to respond. Brian twists in his chair to look at the retreating arachnid, which really is horrendously over-sized, and mutters something indecipherable. Nigel rushes back to our table, saying 'Oh, my goodness, that's a big one, young man' like a Chinese Kenneth Williams, and several other diners stare languorously towards us like somnolent but well-dressed cows.

I catch Jake's eye again. He suddenly looks very young, simultaneously angry and vulnerable – and drop-dead gorgeous – with Angie attached to his arm, close to hysteria, and a red-wine stain spreading across his thigh like blood from a wound.

I fold my napkin and place it on the table, then lean down and slip off one of my Jimmy Choos, standing up with it ready in my hand like a sequinned cosh. I reach up and, with a swift and purposeful blow, bring the flat of the shoe down on the spider, killing it instantly.

As the shoe makes contact with the wall, the sudden single tap sounds like the start of a musical, the aimless, jangling background music seeming to falter and become, just for a moment, the opening bars of *Forty-Second Street*.

Nigel, horrified, starts snapping his fingers to call up an army of waiters further down the pecking order, who rush to our table, deftly delivering bowls of soup and copious apologies. One wipes the black clot of mangled spider off the picture with a dishcloth: it leaves a dark stain. Brian starts in on his soup; the incident seems to have given him an appetite. Angie, whose drama-queen trembling has now subsided, lets go of Jake and sits down again, then immediately regrets it as Jake and I remain standing. He's staring down at his trousers.

'Come with me,' I say, with the authority that comes with experience, moving round the table towards him, taking his arm. 'Cold water will get the worst of it out.'

I guide him firmly away from the table. He is acquiescent, lamblike and dazed, ready to be led. I can feel the contour of his young, muscular arm beneath the cream-coloured sleeve of his jacket: he must work out, I think. I'm aware of Angie's helpless glare boring into my shoulder blades as I head towards the Ladies' Room.

Once there, Jake seems to rouse himself and he hesitates.

'Oh, it's all right,' I say. 'It's an *emergency*. No one will mind.'

Nigel, who has followed us like a Border collie herding sheep, nods vigorously and, grinning like a leering ringmaster, tells us archly that he won't let anyone in until we've quite finished. I open the door and pull Jake inside.

The room is empty, the marble-effect, laminated cubicle doors all open, revealing their *faux* Art Deco interiors. The room always reminds me of a cut-price Titanic.

Jake is uneasy when I tell him to take off his trousers.

'Well, it's either that or I'll have to sponge them down with you still in them,' I say, stepping towards him, hands outstretched.

He blushes again, but no longer looks unnerved. His legs are long and tanned; he could be the eldest son of an American millionaire, an affluent young Turk living on the Med, a film star. He'll scrub up nicely, I think, as I turn on the brass-effect cold water tap at one of the basins and hold his stained trousers beneath the faucet.

'Don't worry. I'll dry them under the hand-dryer,' I say. 'You won't have to go back in looking like you've had an accident.'

The water sparkles as it hits the fabric and breaks up into cherry-red droplets which bounce against the white sink. Jake slips his arms around my waist from behind, pressing himself against me. He smells sweet-sour as a young grape. I can see him in the mirror, his lips pressed against my neck. His hooded eyes look up and meet my gaze.

I watch my reflection smile at his in the gilded mirror.

# ROSIE LUGOSI
## My Dear

Migraines are the best condition I've ever had the good sense to acquire. I only need to wince, palm on side of head, roll my eyes like there's something superglued to my cornea and she leans over and bleats, *oh darling, are you all right?*

'It's okay my dear,' I gasp bravely. 'I think I've got a migraine coming on. Oh fuck.'

Donna gazes at me out of her shining eyes, so full and wet you could scuba dive. Oh those eyes. In her lovely blonde head, on her long cappuccino neck, on her luscious body, a body to die for. To lose myself in.

'It's okay, m'dear. I just need to lie down. Just need my beauty sleep.'

I manage a courageous smile, raise my hand and sweep it gently across my brow, as though the effort at brightness has cost me more than I should have spent.

'You go ahead,' I whisper. 'Philippa and Meg haven't seen you for ages. You'll have a great night.' And they bore me shitless, I think.

'I'll miss you, darling. It's not the same without you.'

'I know, m'dear. I'll ring you in the morning.'

It's my first rule. Never move in, and never let them move in with you. Donna's always respected that. No sighing, dropped hints, innocent conversations about how much cheaper it would be if we split the rent on my fancy warehouse conversion. If she did, I'd be off like a shot. I'm glad she's never tried it on;

she's so gorgeous it'd be a shame to have to dump her.

Sandra from IT was gasping after me from the moment she started back in June. Treat 'em mean and keep 'em keen, say I. Acted like I hadn't noticed for the first month, although I could smell the pheromones pouring off her. She slid off her seat every time I passed by her office. That June, the number of times I found I couldn't access my email you wouldn't believe. Could she help me out? Yes she could.

So, I started dropping in the compliments: *you've got lightning fingers: look how fast you've sorted that out*; and then it was coffee and me doing a lot of laughing at her jokes; then it was a quick drink after work; then it was a slow drink; then it was *you understand me in a way that Donna doesn't*; then it was fucking each other's brains out. I'm never in a hurry. Where's the rush? It's all foreplay, from the first sniff of the quarry.

I only go for the ones that want me. I'm not one of those sad dykes who waste their time mooning over straight women. Give me a break. There's enough queer tottie queueing up out there to keep me occupied till I'm shoving up daisies.

And that's not to mention my gorgeous Donna. The perfect woman: quiet, beautiful, kind, bright but not as bright as me, and fucking loaded. Her father owns a yacht, one of those big bastards you see round the Lido di Jesolo, and that's just for starters. So I'm keeping my feet well under the table. And the most perfect thing of all the perfect things about her? She loves me to distraction.

I plan on keeping it that way. Do I look like a moron? Other women are fun whom I have no intention of giving up, but I'm not coarse about it.

I'm discreet. I treat Donna like a princess: presents, holidays, the works. Can't keep my hands off her. She's crazy about me.

But tonight it's the lovely Sandra. We've been at it for three months now, which is something of a record for me, and therefore time to slap it down. She's been getting the hungry look for a bigger chunk of me than I care to dish up. They all get it, mostly sooner than later; and why not? I'm tall, work out and don't have a face like a bag of spanners like most of the sad sack sisterhood.

Sandra's finished munching (nice orgasm) and is glowing next to me, so dreamily it takes her a while to notice the pained expression I'm laying on. I do the usual stuff about how great it is being with her, make my voice catch until even she'll twig there's something up. Eventually I give up.

'Sandra, there's something on my mind.'

'Mine too.'

Her voice is gaspy, as though she's been holding the words in. Here we go, Jay, I think. *I need you, Jay, I want you.* The number of times I've heard it and it never stops being embarrassing. I hate watching them hurt themselves when I tell them it's over. It always gets me down.

'Yes,' she sighs.

I open my mouth.

'No, let me say it,' she says quickly; puts a finger on my lips. I can smell myself which is quite distracting, so it's a second or two before I hear what she's saying.

'It's been great sex; please don't think I haven't had a great time with you, but I've met someone who means a lot to me. She knows about us, and is cool with it, but I've suddenly realised, um, I want to be with her.'

I discover that my mouth is open, so I shut it. I should be grateful, she's doing the dirty work for me, but all the blood in my head has drained into my stomach.

'I hope you don't take this too badly,' she murmurs, and presses her face into my cheek. I think it's a kiss. I glance down at my breasts and see small vertical stretch marks where they are pulling down from their moorings. I've never noticed them before. I wrap my arms around my chest and scoop my tits upwards. The marks disappear.

Sandra glances at the clock. Three am. I'm out of her bed before she can say anything else, fishing around for my scattered underclothes.

'You can stay,' she says; but I've gathered myself by now, hooking my bra on with my back to her, not remembering at all how she undid it a few hours back.

'No, it's best if I go, Sandra,' I say gravely. 'You're right: it's been fun, and I'm far too big a person to stand between you and the person you love. I do understand.'

It sounds like crap; it is crap, but Sandra laps it up like the idiot she is. Thanks me for being so great. She gets up (all flurried dressing gown now) and makes me a cup of tea, which I don't drink; pours me a whiskey, which I do. It's almost four by the time I get into the taxi she calls me, I have to hang around so long bloody reassuring her that I'm all right. Jesus.

My flat is cold when I get in: all I can think about is Donna. In her lonely bed, loyal and faithful, anxious about my migraine. She does worry. She feels so close to me I imagine I can smell her perfume swirling in the hall. I get into the shower and scrub myself. A couple of hours' sleep, a strong coffee and it'll all feel different. I've already put Sandra behind me. She's due for a transfer anyway. She meant nothing, none of them did. Not like Donna. I'll call her first thing, say I feel better. Tell her I've been thinking; it's time we got somewhere together.

*

Getting her key cut was the easiest thing. Jay keeps a spare one in with the forks; for *emergencies* as she puts it. She didn't notice it disappearing one morning I stayed over. It was back there the next day while she was at work.

I didn't have any clear ideas. To start with, I'd wander from room to room. Hold my hand over the mark in her pillow where her head had been. Pull her long red curls from the plughole in the bath. Lick the stain of her lipstick from the rim of her cup. Sniff the clothes stranded on the bedroom floor. I think I wanted to find signs of them. I never found any, but I knew. From the very first of her 'migraines'. The way she said, *I just need a quiet night in*, I guessed it was the last thing on her mind. I never complained: I laid my hand on hers and said, *would you like me to take care of you?* to make her stay. She always said the same thing, *I just need my beauty sleep*, and touched her forehead as if it hurt to say something funny.

I tried to warn her off: *I'm crazy about you*, I said. *You're the one for me.* I followed her. She didn't go home like she said she was going to but headed straight for their houses. I knew where they lived, the colour of their curtains, how long each affair lasted.

I began sitting in her apartment while she was out with them. I think I wanted her to come home and find me there; wanted the shouting, the fight. But the nights stretched out into months. I sat on her bed, inhaling the air we shared when she was there.

Air tastes different when two people are breathing it.

I left clues for her. A blonde hair on the draining board, my perfume on the hall carpet; stuck my finger inside myself and wiped my scent over her pillowcase. She didn't say anything. Only, *you're so gorgeous, my dear*. At first it was a comfort. *My dear*. The way she called me that. My dear. M'dear. Dear. A sweet little thing. A fawn, a bambi, a bimbo, all big helpless eyes and silky hair.

I wanted to kill her, watch her die. But death would mean she was gone and could feel nothing any more. Death would mean peace for her. That's when it started.

Getting her credit card details was the next thing, so obvious I wonder why I didn't do it first. She even buys coffee with her Visa. I've seen the faces in Starbucks when she whips out her plastic on a Saturday afternoon and the queue is halfway out of the door.

I started small; logged on to Outdoor Traders, picked out a fleece in her size, a buttery golden colour, right for her hair. I rolled the irony around my mouth: a birthday present from me, bought with her money. My fingers stuck to the keys as I typed in her card number and hit Continue. I waited a month for her Visa bill to arrive, for her to moan to me about the rogue transaction. She is good at moaning.

Nothing. I bought myself shoes. A black wig. A Rampant Rabbit. A case of Australian wine. Another case of French white, expensive. Not a word. One morning, when I'd stayed over at hers, the post arrived and she opened it while I was sipping my coffee. I saw the Visa logo at the top of the paper she dragged out of the white envelope; my lips hovered at the brim of my cup. I pretended to blow on the hot liquid. Three sheets of paper. She glanced at the final page, looked surprised, threw it aside and picked up a holiday brochure. A smiling face peered out through the clear plastic wrapper. I couldn't help myself.

'You look surprised, darling.'

'Only my Visa bill, m'dear. Less than I expected. Always a nice surprise. I only ever pay off the minimum. Life's too short.'

I loved her. So maybe I am a dumb blonde. Her lion's mane of russet curls, the way her teeth glittered when she laughed, which was often. Her lazy smile, her lazy walk, the way she put her hands into me. The parade of other women through her eyes, the smell of new brine on her fingers, the mark of other mouths on her when she kissed me. Imagining all the other ears that heard her say *oh God* when she closes her eyes and lets go.

I forgot myself the once, bit her while she was lying on top of me, panting like a Dobermann. Fixed my teeth into the pulse in her neck, tasted the rust of her blood. She yipped, sprang up onto her elbows. I could feel heat flare in my limbs, I was so close to losing myself and tearing her into shreds.

'My little dear has teeth,' she laughed, and went back to thrusting into me. I thought of garnet necklaces. Black stockings with red seams. Shoes with heels sharp as knives. What I would buy next. But pretty things left me empty.

It was the computer that gave me the idea. Every time I bought something, bright windows popped up, clamoured for my attention; enticing me to visit other websites. Sites where men fucked women. Fed me links to more and more and more; where women fucked women; men fucked men. If she'd come home to me, I would have stopped there.

The police track hundreds of people through their

credit card details. It's only a matter of time before they get to her and confront her with the other purchases I started making.

I don't look at the screen, the frail child bodies made grotesque. Girls, always girls. After all, it's what the gutter press say we do. I concentrate on the keys. Will myself not to look at the pictures. I drag the cursor over the website name, click the mouse, delete it from History. It's still on the hard drive, an easy thing to find for those who know how to search. Festering deep inside with all its foul companions, each one I've logged on to month after month, every time she's claimed another migraine and gone to fuck her latest woman. Impossible to erase. Easy to trace, along with the vile images bought with her credit card.

I switch off, wait for the screen to wink out, pull a screen wipe over the mouse and keys. Rub at my fingers. Three am. I pause by her front door and spray perfume behind my ears.

# BREN LUCAS

## Reader, I Mullered Him

'Mullered': *Adj.* slang for state of drunkenness,
or insobriety brought about by drugs. In
football parlance: issuing a big defeat on your
opponents; to play the other team off the field.

You'd know him if you saw him walking down the
street, recognise him from the posters and ad
campaigns he's fronted, though probably you'd know
him best of all from the papers and the television. It's
possible you might even have seen him playing,
wearing that pristine white 38 when he couldn't keep
his usual 11 after he was transferred. He's Bee Jay the
BJ; Bee Jay the Ball Jock, or Bee Jay the Ball Jenius.
The comedians came up with that last one, playing
on the fact he's not so articulate and, what with the
thick accent, he doesn't come across as all that sharp.
But it's not only because of his exploits on the pitch
that the initials stuck. It's as much for what he likes
off it, when he's playing by himself, one against one,
no team to back him up. Well, not usually. But you'll
have read all about that in the papers, in big type and
banner headlines.

BJ, he swears he's going straight now, a married
man, with a little one on the way. Gonna be a daddy.
This Saturday lunchtime there's a television feature
all about him, filmed in the big conservatory of his
Liverpool mansion. All about the way he's kicked his
demons, given up 'roasting', learned the love of a good
woman, understands how lucky he is to be where he
is, doing what he does best of all in all the world,
enjoying his football before it's too late. A changed

character, he was saying. Getting himself straight.

Aw. Bless.

You look at his eyes, the way they get all big and earnest when the camera goes in for a close-up, you could almost believe him.

Only not tonight. Tonight he's not thinking about his wife and the forthcoming arrival. With the spinning multi-coloured lights swirling across his shirt, the pounding music like the beat of a drum, the press of flesh against flesh – and all of it his to choose from – his thoughts are anywhere but at home with the expectant mother. And him having just done the TV show. How hypocritical is that?

Maybe because this is a small town hidden up in the North he thinks there's gonna be no one around to tell on him. Wrong again, buster.

Still, at least it's not hard to get his attention. My hair's freshly highlighted and straightened, and what naturally wouldn't go all the way down to my bum does so with the extensions. They weren't cheap, and I got them out of the money for my last job. But they say you've got to speculate to accumulate, and I like accumulating.

The hair's good in more ways than one. It's a kind of misdirection, a dummy before a swift side-shuffle past the defender. And even if he were keeping an eye out for me, warned by his boss, he still wouldn't expect me looking like this. Hair doesn't grow that quickly, he'd think. If he was thinking with his head at all.

They really aren't the brightest, these guys.

Rich, yes.

But bright?

Do me a favour.

In this tight little dress my dad says hardly qualifies, I stride across to him, slinking my hips and tensing the muscles in my legs, not an ounce of excess fat to be seen in the wrong places. I'm looking at no one else but him all the way, little pout on my lips, but not too much of one because you don't want to overdo it. With my chin tilted down, I'm giving him the doe-eyes as I come, showing him how submissive I can be, even though my body language is telling him just what I want, so he can't fail to get the message.

I'm making that *perfectly* clear.

When I do my walk this sea of people just parts, opening up wide and easy, just how it must be for him when he's bearing down on goal and he can't miss scoring. For a moment I think I know what it must be like to *be* him, can imagine the screams and cheers as everyone in the stadium around him holds their breath, and him soaking it all in while everything climaxes.

With the people moving aside in the nightclub it gives me a chance to stretch my legs, so he can see just how long they are, all the way from my heels up to where the dress barely starts. My little handbag, a piece of heaven from Prada you wouldn't believe the price of, is there bumping at my right hip, and I'm glad of its weight, a little reassurance in case I come close to losing my nerve. But I never do. I think of my family, think of everyone who's counting on me, and it's a matter of pride that I get the job done.

BJ's drinking, propped up against a round table near the bar, with a couple of lads hanging around him. His entourage: all gelled hair and off-the-peg shirts, high street trousers and socks they've bought from the big stores. Not so the man himself – it's strictly top-class designer goods for him, from the cut of his shirt to the James Dean trousers he bragged about buying at some snazzy auction. There's a gold chain around his wrist, setting off his watch, a big chunky affair that's probably a genuine Rolex and not bought off a Greek beach like my dad's was for a fiver. And there's his wedding ring, covered in blue tape, like it was when he was playing in the cup game this afternoon.

I spotted BJ as soon as he came through the door with his crowd of mates, none of them football players far as I know; just like a king and his followers, the hangers-on hoping for any scraps he might drop their way. Recognised him from the car advert he used to do before he was caught drunk-driving, this big sports coupé lost in the country lanes, kids smiling at him as he passes by, taking the long route back home from a game (where he's naturally scored) because the car is such a pleasure to drive. His hair's not the same as in the ad, receded a bit, but he's got it shorter now, combed forward in an expensive cut so you wouldn't notice how much it's thinned.

And I've had my eye on him ever since, waiting for the moment to make my move. It's not just luck I'm here, but there was always the chance he wouldn't be – or come to that any of his team-mates that I could take as substitutes, though it's pointless doing it with some nobody who's only ever kicked a ball once. The papers want the stars you've all heard about. And they're the hardest to get. It's where I've made my reputation, though. I'm in another league; it's why I'm on first-name terms with the tabloid editors.

I heard about the nightclub from this website that tells you where the best in the country are. Only the top places. Where there's a really tough door policy and you don't get in unless you look the part. Ones where the local celebs hang out. The hardest bit's getting past the bouncers, but one glance at you should be enough if you're not too gobby or needy and look like you belong. One of my brothers works in the café with the computers in Sheffield city centre, knows his way around them, so he shows me what to look for on the Web, how to find the places and then what they want on the door. It's amazing the stuff you can learn off the Internet. If someone's visiting a new town or city and they've got money, they're always gonna go to the biggest clubs, check out the local talent. So I look to where the biggest teams are playing and then hunt down those exclusive nightclubs, try to make sure that that talent's me.

You wouldn't think an off-the-map town like this would have such a big nightclub, would you? Not an exclusive one, anyway. But here I am, all the same; here we all are, swinging to the music in the near dark. And I'm ready to play to my rules.

It's funny, but I never really realised some people might think what I do is wrong. It's my body and I can do what I like with it. I've never done topless shots, for instance, even when this paper offered me a lot of money. I've done shots in knickers and bra, but that was to go with an article about me; and I've never shown any nipple. Don't think my mum would mind, but I'm not sure about my dad. He can be funny that way. Sometimes, the way I see him looking at me . . . He's proud of me, of course. Like my mum. Well, when your little girl's been in the paper so often, had double-page spreads about her, and her only coming from a terrace house in the back streets of Sheffield where there was no money when she was growing up, it's understandable. They call Dad Mr Eyre on the street now, whereas before it was always Dave – 'Ay up, Dave.' But now he's got respect. 'Afternoon, Mister Eyre.' And all because of me.

But thinking about my dad now's not right. I've got work to do, so I relegate those thoughts and concentrate on the game.

What I've done, since he came into the nightclub – I've made sure to catch BJ's eye a couple of times. I was dancing by myself, just marking time, and when some nobody came along and tried to dance with me, I'd just tell them to fuck off, spin away and leave them standing. I'd already seen a big guy by himself, drinking at the corner of the bar. So I'd point him out, tell anyone who was too insistent and wouldn't go away that I was with him and if they wanted to argue the case go see him about it. No one did and I soon got the space back to myself. Meant I could look BJ's direction now and again, keep an eye on him, see him seeing me through the crowd. But I didn't go over to him too soon. It was hard to turn my back on him, I'll admit, just dance, then glance his way once in a while. You've got to time it right, though, gotta lose your marker and go in for the kill at the exact moment, else you get flagged and you've missed your chance.

So I've caught his eye, danced while he watched me, waited for the right time; and now the walk's done, clubbers parted like the sea for Moses, and I'm there in front of BJ, just a few feet from the table, right on the cusp, showing him the cargo and how it's all his if he shows me something back. I know I look hot. I didn't need a boob job to make this outfit look good, not the way his wife did so she'd fit the dresses you see her in. I work out, you know, but I'm natural too, started off with the right genes. All I'm doing is enhancing what was there to begin with. I spend my money on me, looking good, making it so I can go out again and make more money. The amount I can earn from this one job, it's more than most girls round our street see in three years. Down the salon, there's girls my age and they're not even making minimum wage yet. It's like when I go in for my hair or something, I'm a celebrity. They all know me, what I do, from the papers. And they always give me the best manicure, spend the longest time on my styling; they understand how important it all is and I can see them wishing they were me.

And yeah, from the way BJ's looking at me I can tell all that work's done the trick. He's trying not to show he's impressed, but I know I've had him interested since we first made eye contact. For all that, though, I know I've still gotta make him come for me these last few steps. He's had enough girls flinging themselves his way over the evening, and he's nodded and flirted with a few – I've seen him leaning over so they can shout their offers in his ear over the sound of the music – but they all hang around too much, crowding him, and he soon makes it clear he's not interested.

He could have his pick, anything off the rack. But like his clothes, he wants designer, he wants exclusive, made-to-measure. To get that you've got to go further than stand round a table and have it thrust on you. Designer, *you* go after.

I strike a pose in front of him and his mates, looking at BJ only, just to make sure he knows no one else in the room exists apart from the two of us; and his eyes haven't left mine since I made my walk. I'm excited, nervous all over. But I can't let it show. Sometimes, moments like this, I think I can hear the girls in the salon cheering me on, wanting to read all about it in the papers, and there's this mantra running in my head that I can't shake off: *Don't blow it, don't blow it, don't blow it.*

I've done all I can up to here. He's either gonna go for it tonight or he's not. All I can do is wait for him to blow the whistle to start the game or end it.

And for a moment I think BJ's not gonna move. There's just this beat, a heartbeat, where he stays sitting and I feel like such a fool, thinking about the train fare gone down the tube, how I've come here to this club and now I'm gonna have to find some guy I can wank off in a minute for a night's sleep on a bed somewhere or else stump up myself for a hotel room.

I don't let it show, how big a deal it is if BJ's not interested, though. Wouldn't give him the satisfaction. I'll just smile his way, turn around and walk off, knowing he's watching my bum and the slick muscles down my back all the while I head out of his life.

And then, just as I'm about to give him the smile and turn around, he stands up, ignoring what one of his mates is shouting in his ear above the music, handing him his glass. The look on his mate's face is priceless as he's left standing there like he's nothing, puzzled why he's being ignored. He's a guy who knows his place, though, and just shrugs it off when he sees me and realises he's been passed over. He's already sipping BJ's beer as compensation. Pond life.

But it's BJ I'm interested in. He's slinky, taller than I thought he'd be, and I like the idea of his body all over me, having him hard and wanting me. I think of him stripping me bare and running his tongue down my body. He's a guy who's on TV every week, and you read about him in the papers every other day. And it's just gonna be me and him, just in one small room. I'll have him all to myself. All those other girls who wanted him, they're blown out of the water. Just for me.

That's ego on my part, I know, a little perk of the job. I'm gonna fake it no matter how good he isn't. Would do even if he'd put the weight on again, like he did after his injury and he had trouble getting back in shape. But you never know, there's always the possibility you'll find one who doesn't think sex is just a main course you've gotta gulp down as soon as you get to the table.

It's not happened yet, but it might one day. You'd think their wives would teach them, wouldn't you? But they never seem to. Least, the players I've been with never seem to have learned anything. I wonder sometimes, about the married ones, if it's just that they don't have to worry about anyone but themselves in a situation like this. I'd like to ask one of the wives one day. Maybe they do only marry for the money and want the sex over as soon as possible. Some of the ones I've been with, it's a mercy it is over so quickly.

BJ's coming closer, and he smiles at me, says in his Scouse accent, 'You wan' in' some'ing?'

I smile back, but not to make it too obvious I spin him on a bit. 'Way you were looking at me, I thought you were the one wanting something.'

'Yeah? What's this "some'ing", then?'

'Don't you know?'

'I know wor it is *I* mean.'

'Maybe it's the same thing I do. Saw you there and thought from the way you're looking, *There's a man who wants something.*'

I know he's mine soon as he grins back at his mates, gives them a quick wave. The music throbs but to me it's like it's all gone away, at a remove from the two of us; there's only him and me in the eye of this hurricane, spectator sport as far as everyone else is concerned.

I tug under the lapel of his shirt to get his attention back, getting a little possessive, showing him it's just him I'm interested in. 'What's the problem? Can't handle it by yourself?'

He leans forward to speak into my ear, and I tilt my head for him to do so, letting him smell the perfume I sprayed there in the loos a few minutes ago. 'Do yer knows who I am?' he says.

I smile, teasing, then lean up to speak in his ear, smelling a mix of alcohol and expensive cologne that he's splashed too much of on all over. 'Sorry, but if you don't know, yourself, I can't help you . . .'

He tells me he's a football player and I tell him 'Oh, yeah?' like I don't believe it.

It's not the most articulate and passionate conversation I've ever had. But you've gotta play it on their level. You can't discuss books and things in a nightclub, not that I'm a big reader, even though I'm supposed to have a famous namesake in a novel. I tell him I don't watch football, that I've never met a real player before. He tells me his name and I tell him he can't be him.

'Prove it,' I say. 'Show me your hotel room.'

And it's as simple as that.

He's got a room in the grandest place in town, of course, one that's not far from the nightclub. A hotel called the Rochester. Sadly there's every prospect of walking, because it's so close, which I'm not too happy about because it's cold now and I've not got much on and in these heels would definitely have preferred a taxi. He points out people watching him as he's recognised on the streets, proving who he is to me. I laugh and let him think I think he's kidding me on. The room's not the biggest I've ever been in, but it's one of the highest up. I stand by the window as he raids the minibar, just looking beyond my reflection at all the lights out there.

'Ere,' he says, coming up from behind and looping a hand around me, squeezing my left breast so hard it hurts, merging his reflection with mine and pressing up against me. There's a bottle in his other hand, a small one, still with a faint chill of the fridge clinging to it. I don't even get a glass, I mean that much to him. But that's all right, it's business on my part as well. He leans closer, and his voice vibrates through me as he puts his lips on my neck and speaks. 'Drink up, will yer,' he says and it hurts again as he squeezes in what he must think is a provocative way. 'Come on to bed wiv me, yeah?'

I'm not gonna drink from that bottle, but I take it anyway, turning around so that we're face to face. I can feel the cold glass against my back as he presses me against the window. You don't know what might be in the drinks, what they might have put in them, so I put the bottle aside as quickly as I can without making it obvious, then make sure he knows he's getting what he wants anyway, drink or no drink.

'Show me your bed and I'll think about it.'

He snorts, happy, peals away, holding me by the hand. 'S over 'ere.'

He's disgusting, despite him being on the telly and in the papers, and for a moment I almost think I won't go through with it. But then I remember I've been here before and how the world looks different from the other end of a cheque for the night's work. He's talking about today's game, the FA Cup and how they're through to the next round. All the while I guide him over to the bed, pushing his chest to get him there. His paws are all over me and he's lost his own drink somewhere – I think I heard him drop it on the carpet, but can't be sure because the pile's so thick – and he hurts my right boob this time as he paws at me, so that I have to twist away and make it sound like a laugh that escapes me and not a gasp of pain. He's using football language that I pretend not to know about, terms of the game, diving, blind referees, foreigners invading the league and moaning he couldn't get his number 11 shirt cos some Italian had it already, having to wear a poxy 38 cos the 3 and the

8 add up to 11. He's actually a lot drunker than I'd thought, and I worry for a while that he's gonna get violent.

He puts a bruise on me and I'm going to the police.

But I don't want to draw him on the violence front – it's not even worth the compensation of having him up in court, so I try to keep things lighter. Some guys, you never can tell. They think all women are responsible for something they reckon one woman did to them years ago. Screwed up losers. I let him take me the last steps toward the bed, just so he knows he's gonna be happy, think he's in control.

I make sure my handbag's where I left it, nearby on the bedside cabinet, and then I let him strip me. He's not really too well co-ordinated, but he gets the job done eventually, sucking on my breasts as he shuffles my dress down and then starts nosing at my knickers. I stop him and take his shirt off, and his pants, then I let him go down and take mine off too. We're both naked then, and a bit of me's always slightly excited that I've turned on someone like him from the telly, even if he is just like all the others. I roll away from him on the bed, get the handbag as he's asking me wor I'm doing, pull out a condom to show him. And he's not happy with that. But the way he is now, he doesn't argue too much when I put it in my mouth and beckon him over with a finger. Slipping it on over him, unrolling it and sheathing him, I then stay there, tonguing him where he likes, letting him live up to his name, his initials, till he bucks and groans and gushes safely into the rubber.

After that he's a bit slower, not too quick about anything, and ready to sleep. He's already forgotten about me. He doesn't even care that I wrap the condom tight and tie it up, saving it for later, evidence in case he wants to contest anything.

I wait till he's snoring, then get up, find my handbag. I fish out my Nokia cell phone and check the charge and memory capacity, even though I'd done so before I came out tonight, then make sure the photo lens is clean and that I'm getting a decent picture. It's all looking good, and the hotel room lights are bright enough for what I need, so I pad back to the bed, pull the sheets away, revealing him lying there naked. He's so far gone he doesn't notice. I take a few shots with the Nokia, sure to get his face on the screen. Then I have some fun, dressing him in my knickers and taking more pictures of him in one of the complimentary dressing gowns. 'Hers', of course.

When I've done, I double-check the pictures are clear and you can recognise him, that I've stored them properly on the phone. Opening his wallet, I take out the train fare from a stash of fifties he keeps behind a picture of his wife, and then I get dressed. I'm already on the mobile before the door's closed and I'm out of his hotel room, going through the numbers in the memory. I ring them all, the usual editors I know the first names of, and ask them to start the bidding for my story and pictures.

The one who stumps up the most money asks if I thought twice about selling BJ down the tube, for getting him in trouble with his pregnant wife so soon after his television interview. I know he's joking when he asks, and like it that he calls me 'Jane' or 'love' like my dad does and not 'Janey'. I tell him if it hadn't been me tonight, it would have been someone else. You've gotta take your chances when you can, put the ball in the back of the net. He laughs at that.

I look back at the closed hotel room door, think of BJ sleeping it off, not even knowing what the morning's gonna bring him. And you know what? It's true: I don't care; he's had what he wanted and now I'm getting what I want.

The editor's telling me the headlines he's gonna run, on account of it all happening in the Rochester and my name being the same as this famous character from a book. I don't get it, but so what? It's the money that counts. I just laugh and tell him it's great when he says, 'How d'you like this one, Jane? Right across the front page:

'Reader, I mullered him.'

'Just so long as you spell my name right on the cheque, Edward, I'm anyone's,' I say, and, to the echo of his laughter, head inside the lift, going down. The doors close and make a sound like a whistle blowing full time.

# LYNNE TAYLOR
## Big Bad Momma

I look long and hard at the woman in the mirror. I'm quite fond of her. Always felt respect. She's very much her own person. Pleases no one but herself.

That person is about to disappear.

Here goes. I peel off my shirt, jeans. Ugh. But for thirty-five it could be worse. I'm still a size ten. Just. I squeeze myself into a piece of lycra that could optimistically be called a top. Black of course. And a neckline that's far too low. But he likes them like that. Then the skirt: a long slashed satin affair with bits of net stuck on. Holy Moses. But no way am I going for the mini.

Now for the boots. Good thing she's my size. God, they're heavy. How does she walk in these? Soles must be an inch thick. I lace them to the top; half way up my shin. Well hey! Now I know how she walks. Feel invincible! Could kill for Britain in these!

Where's the belt? Here. Mandatory black, chunky and silver studded, with a sheath. I bought that. They dress like they're going to war these days.

Now for the make-up. If you're a true goth the eyes have to be black, the face pale and the lips as deep purple as they can get. This is looking good. Hardly know myself. But my hair is blonde and short. No good. Has to be long and black and looking like it had a fight with a rainbow. So, this is one I prepared earlier; a long black wig. I stretch it over my head, tuck wispy bits of me out of sight. Fantastic. Mustn't forget the spray. Could only find green and pink but they'll do. I lift a tuft at the front and spray shocking pink. I lift a clump from round the back and add lurid green.

Now the *pièce de résistance*; black lace gloves. I pull them on; long, long, elbow deep. He likes that too: the ultra feminine with the aggressively male.

Oh     my     God.   Can that be me?

I creep down the stairs, sneak out the back. Taxi? No. Take the car. Won't need more than one drink, music will do the rest. It does that to me, rock: I get high off it.

He'll be there. I know he'll be there.

There's a band on tonight: Big Bad Momma. They do have this thing about mothers, these heavy metal guys: motherfucker this, motherfucker that. Together with skulls and blood and guts. The mother in me thinks they glorify violence, but maybe it's just a healthy release of teeming virility.

Where was I? Oh yes, this band. He loves them. Loves the really heavy stuff. Goes apeshit when he moshes. I have to give it to the guy, when he moves, something in me moves with him. And the same goes for a hell of a lot of women.

I enter the club, 'enter' being the operative word. You don't go in, you enter this other world.   Been coming for years with my mates but I'm normally a jeans and T-shirt woman. Not tonight. Not like last time when I brought Rose. *Go on, Mum,* she said. *I go in pubs all the time*!  I knew she did, and I knew she was a good kid, so I thought, *why not?* We'd said, once we're in, we do our own thing. Never thought a daughter of mine would like rock too. Perhaps she had no choice.  But that's a good thing about rock; you get all kinds of people, all ages.

Inside it is perpetual night: degrees of darkness that thickens in corners. There is an aura of anticipation, a sense of destiny.  Everything waits, passive, the music a back-drop.  I thread myself through bodies towards the bar.

'Pint, please.'

'Comin' up!'

Excellent. Normally he says, *Usual*? And I say, *Please*.

My eyes adjust to the dark, scan the crowd.

He is here.

His eyes graze faces: skims mine, goes past, comes back. Gives me the once-over. Knew he would.

I turn away and mutter something banal to the guy next to me. But make it plain we are not an item. That's another thing. All this macho stuff but everybody's friendly.

The bar isn't an intrusion, a focus, it is purely fundamental; a steady flow of frothing beer as the night deepens. Places fill, pints breed: empty glasses, full glasses, people glazed.

Big Bad Momma take the stage. *They* are the focus.

Music stirs like a dormant beast, prowls, the throb throbbing; insistent. Expectancy curls like an opium haze, ripples with the prescience of arousal, pulsating, restless. Heads turn, bodies tense, flames of music spiral from a space, beckon like a magnet, calling, *this way, here . . .*

Legs are galvanised, black leathered, move, or lissom, short-skirted, glide towards the source, music coiled tighter, tighter, springs, thrusts from its lair, tongue flames licking, incites: exciting. Boots bounce, bodies sway, twist, rock, heads lolling, hair flying, reel, the beast flaunting itself, brazen, louder, a spirit unleashed, spearing, jumping, a dervish whirling, lashing faster, crashing, let it come, bashing, deep inside, thrashing, let go, smashing . . .

The singer whispers hoarsely through the mike:

'You want some more?'

'Yeah!'

'I said, d'you want some more?'

'Yeah!'

'D'YOU WANT SOME FUCKING MORE?'

'YEAH!'

And we rock, lashing faster, crashing, let it come, and as I move and sway I slink between bodies, nearly there, and spin, whirly spin, spinning whirl, hair flying until I'm here, eyes connect, lock – we grin, moving closer, music rocking, louder, rocking, louder, rocking, do it, louder, not yet, louder, harder, louder.

YES!

Arms punch the air.

I thrust the knife

     in

          hilt deep

with a slight resistance like the skin of an orange. A blood orange.

He roars. They all roar. And no one sees so I turn and slip through bodies slumping, heaving, slowing, spent, and someone SHOUTS.

There are splinters of screams.

I weave away as people spread like a ripple from a stone in a pool. There's no stone in the middle of this pool. Just a body. Not a heaving one, a dead one, sprawled, blood oozing like a flower, a red one, a rose.

I slip into the silk of the night.

Here's one mother you won't fuck.

And there'll be no more daughters you'll rape.

Motherfucker.

# SOPHIE HANNAH

# I Deeply and Completely Love Myself

My sister once said to me, 'You wouldn't ever kill anyone, would you? Or, you know, have someone killed?' A comic slant to her voice indicated that she was prepared to be indulgent, whatever my answer turned out to be. She is commendably loyal. It was nine o'clock on a Friday evening, and we were sitting in my lounge, drinking mulled wine. My twins were asleep upstairs. Dom and Ed, my husband and Sally's boyfriend, were in the pub, and Sally and I seized the opportunity to have a conversation that did not contain the words 'crampon' or 'European constitution'.

It was an important question, one I hadn't been asked before, and one to which I would have liked to give serious consideration before answering. At the same time, I was aware that it was not the sort of matter one ought to need to think about, so I quickly said, 'No', then realised that it wasn't as simple as that. If, say, I were to be diagnosed with a terminal illness and given only a year to live, I might risk it, if the arguments in favour were persuasive enough. If the disincentive of long-term loss of liberty were to be taken out of the equation . . .

I say long-term because I've often thought a short spell behind bars would be quite relaxing. I've taken film crews into several prisons over the years, and I think it's an environment that might suit me. There wouldn't be two small babies in my cell waking me up every hour and a half, wailing for bottles of milk. There would be no tearing round the world with microphones and cameras and lighting equipment while simultaneously trying to run a home and a family. I wouldn't have to shop, cook, do the laundry or co-ordinate my seventeen-strong pool of babysitters and nannies, the team that looks after Dom and the twins when I'm working away. Apart from the obligatory hour-a-day spent marching round the concrete yard in an orange plastic jumpsuit and leg-irons, glowering at butch and corrupt guards, all my time would be my own, to be filled with reading, thinking, imagining, dreaming – real 'me-time', as the women's magazines call it. All right, so I'd only be allowed two outfits and they'd both be ugly and practical, but would that necessarily be any more depressing than spending a fortune on designer knitwear only to have it vomited and weed on daily by one's nearest and dearest?

As with most things, there are pros and cons. I wouldn't want my children to have to live with my bad reputation after I was dead. I found it hard enough, as a child, to deal with my peers having seen my mother's rainbow-striped wellington boots. She'd found them in a wire-mesh basket outside Crick's, the hardware shop that always smelled of bleach, and thought they were 'a jolly good bargain' at only a pound. I didn't want to inflict an even worse shame upon my own offspring. (My mother, incidentally, misunderstood me when, after my last trip to a prison, I told her I thought I'd adjust quite well if ever I did get sent down. In her world, being sent down means being expelled from either Oxford or Cambridge University. It is possible that, as Mum suggested as kindly as she could, I have spent too much time consorting romantically with the lower orders. As a teenager and in my early twenties, I sought out the scabby, the pock-marked, the inarticulate, as a way of rebelling against my upper-middle-class parents. But my question is this: what use is a Cheltenham Ladies' College and Newnham education if one ends up buying crap wellies from a metal bucket for a quid?)

'No,' I said again, more firmly. 'I don't think I'd ever kill anyone.'

'Good. Hope you don't mind me asking.' Sally laughed. 'It's just that . . . well, I wouldn't *entirely* put it past you!'

I tried to look outraged, but secretly I was flattered that she regarded me as somebody not to be messed with. This is because I keep a long list in my head of all the people who have messed with me quite extensively over the years. For someone who claims to take no shit, I seem to have taken an awful lot, if my accounting is accurate. Perhaps that's why I'm so vocal about my grudges: because time after time people treat me badly and I do nothing about it (see references to Carl later in anecdote). Or I retaliate, but only after years, sometimes decades, of being a doormat (see references to Roberta later in anecdote).

Feeling suddenly as if my enemies had got off scot-free, I added, 'If I did kill someone, though, it'd be either (here come those references) Carl or Roberta. And I'd do it myself. I wouldn't hire a hit-man. I'd probably try to push them off something high. I don't think I could do anything like stabbing. Maybe I'd run them over.' Now I felt even more ineffectual. The quiet ones, it is commonly agreed, are always the worst, and I am not a quiet one. I am all talk. My death threats are just empty posturing.

'Why kill Carl?' asked Sally.

'Well, I don't especially want to . . . but that's because I'm waiting for an apology. I think that'll still be true in twenty years. If I thought he was never going to apologise, it'd be a different matter.'

'He's never going to apologise.' Sally sighed. She'd said this dozens of times before. 'He was so massively out of order, he can't afford to admit it. No one says, "Yes, you're quite right – I'm a complete shit. Well done for spotting what a tosser I am and drawing it to my attention." '

'He could say, "I *was* a complete shit."'

'But he isn't going to. He's not rational. He's so screwed up, he just lashes out, then invents the justification later. We've been over this.'

'Hm.' I frowned. 'If what you say is true, then that means he still thinks I'm the one to blame.'

'So?'

'That's a reason to kill him. I don't like the idea of his . . . consciousness existing if it's going to think something so blatantly unfair about something that's so important to me.'

Sally groaned. 'He shouldn't *be* important to you. He never should have been. You're *married*. Just forget about him.' Just forgetting about Carl was an excellent idea. It was right up there alongside Lady Macbeth being less ambitious and Michael Moore trying really hard to play nicely with George Bush.

A couple of weeks earlier, I had been to see an emotional freedom therapist, hoping she would be able to treat my continuing obsession with Carl, the injustice, his abandonment of me. She asked me to hum *Happy Birthday* with her. This was only the preamble. Later, she said, she would require me to tap my eyebrow, cheekbone and armpit, among other bodily parts, and chant 'Even though I still care what Carl thinks, I deeply and completely love myself.' I told her I couldn't do it, not any of it, not even the humming of *Happy Birthday*. Especially not the humming. She said it didn't have to be *Happy*

*Birthday*; it could be any song that we both knew. As if that would make all the difference. Did she honestly believe I was going to say, 'Oh, well, in *that* case, if we can hum *Pour Some Sugar on Me* by Def Leppard, I absolutely retract all my objections'?

'It's very effective,' she said. 'All my patients say that whatever's bothering them bothers them a lot less immediately after the tapping.'

'I'm sure that's true,' I said. 'But at the moment, however miserable I feel, I believe Carl's wrong to hate me, if he does. The minute I start prodding my eye socket and chanting, chances are I'll begin to think he's got a point.'

To Sally I said, 'Isn't it interesting? The two people I'd be keenest to kill – one's someone I love and one's someone I hate.'

'You don't love Carl,' Sally said patiently, in the same tone she'd have used to tell Sisyphus not to bother with the silly rock. 'You never did.'

'I agree, there are better reasons to kill Roberta.'

'No, there aren't,' said Sally. I was beginning to suspect she had a hidden agenda: she was totally biased in favour of my never murdering anybody. 'She can't do you any harm. You've made your stand. You don't see her, she has nothing to do with the twins.'

'At the moment. But what about when they're older? I can't stop her contacting them as adults, and filling their heads with poison. And don't think she'll be too old and frail by then. People like her live till they're about three hundred, consolidating their evil empires and cackling until their bones turn to a fine, toxic powder.'

The front door opened. Dom and Ed stomped in, blowing on their red hands and shaking their heads, fresh from a row about the European constitution (Dom is anti, Ed is pro).

'What have you girls been talking about?' Ed asked Sally. He tried to sound good-humoured, but he couldn't help eyeing me suspiciously. He is constantly afraid I will embroil Sally in vicious and unsalubrious dissections of innocent bystanders. I try to oblige whenever I can.

'Roberta the reptile,' I said.

Roberta is my father's second wife, though they're in the process of divorcing. She is a woman whose ego can only rest easy if she is surrounded by the misery of others. She is kind to the unhappy and the unfortunate, but cannot stand anybody who seems too cheerful or confident. I obviously fitted the bill, because from the moment my father introduced us, Roberta started making subtly snide remarks, each of which, individually, might not have been meant maliciously. Things like, 'I don't think it's possible to work in the media these days and have any integrity. Oops, sorry, Jane!' And, 'My boss has got such *terrible* skin – she looks as if she's got leprosy. I mean, *much* worse than yours, Jane.' I think I had two small spots at the time.

Once we were at the theatre and I bumped into an old school friend, Leonie Cullen. As a child she'd resembled a boy, and as an adult she looked like a man. Specifically, she looked like Dan Conner from *Roseanne*. (I say this not to be cruel but to set the scene for Roberta's next atrocity.) After we'd chatted for a few minutes, I returned to Dom, Sally, Ed, my father and his still-relatively-new wife. While the others argued vigorously about the play, Roberta leaned over and whispered in my ear, 'You looked really pretty when you were standing next to Leonie.' I turned to face her, amazed. She smiled the meek, virtuous smile of a humble soul who'd just paid the sweetest of compliments to a much-loved stepdaughter.

Whenever I tell anyone about Roberta, I give a few examples of her spitefulness and then say, 'That's just a taster. There are thirty billion other double-edged digs I could report, but we'd be here all day.' For years, she jabbed away with her nasty little insinuations. I used to count them; the average score was four cruel comments per social occasion, although sometimes there were none and once, when I spent a whole weekend with her, there were thirty-two. If I ever raised an eyebrow in shock or puzzlement, she would say, 'Oh, I didn't mean it like *that*.' And then, with relish, 'Oh *dear*! I haven't upset you, have I? I have, haven't I?' Then she would insist on trying to hug me and murmur soothing reassurances, as if I were a poor thing who needed her support in order to face the world.

Astonishingly, I put up with this treatment for nearly ten years, thinking that, since she made sure these verbal attacks were never witnessed, I would be unable to prove anything. Then one day I realised that there was no scheduled court hearing; I did not need to persuade twelve angry men, or even twelve amiable women. The only person who needed to be convinced was me, and, boy, was I convinced. I have more doubts about the Marquis de Sade's cruel streak than I do about Roberta's.

Ed looked hurt. 'Don't call her a reptile,' he said.

Sally is very close to my father, closer than I am, so she and Ed used to see a lot of him and Roberta. What Ed doesn't know is that Sally agrees with me about Roberta, not with him, but she keeps quiet for my dad's sake, and now for Ed's. When Ed lost his job, Roberta gave him some money and stuck close by him in his misery. 'Dejection! Desolation! Let me get my spindly hands on it!' – I swear I saw the words glowing in her brain.

Sally and Ed still see Roberta, even now that she and Dad have separated. People keep telling me that the crumbling old witch is part of the family, as if that means one ought to overlook all salient characteristics. Part of the family! I don't know how Primrose Shipman feels, but that line cuts no ice with me.

I knew Ed had been in the pub for three hours and often got emotional when he'd had a few pints; I shouldn't have provoked him. 'Not a reptile, then,' I said. 'An arachnid. A ghoul. A pox.' I just couldn't help it. It amused me to point out a glaringly obvious truth and have it objected to as if it were a pernicious lie. I felt as if I'd walked into a Marx Brothers movie, as one of the normal people who are treated as risible deviants by the lunatic protagonists.

White and red patches appeared on Ed's cheeks, and his lips thinned. 'You're the horrible one,' he yelled at me. 'Roberta never says anything derogatory about you. All she ever says is that she wishes you could be friends, and wishes she could see the twins. You don't even *know* her! It's arrogant to pretend you do. What, so you saw her a couple of times a week during the nineties? Big deal!'

Dom sighed and turned on the news. I knew what he was thinking: why do we have to go over this again, when there are best routes over Snowdon and referenda to fight about? Dom thought Roberta was a depraved harpy, but most of the time he couldn't remember why; the detail escaped him.

Now it was Sally's turn to get angry, with Ed. 'Why do you *always* have to misrepresent yourself?' she said. 'That's *not* what you think. Whenever we discuss it, you say you can *see* that Roberta's treated Jane badly, and you *don't* think it's all Jane's fault.'

I raised my hand to hide a smile. Every time Ed

does or says something that's not ideal, Sally accuses him of misrepresenting himself. This is another feature of her loyalty; she cannot bear the thought that others might not see the Ed she knows and loves, so she edits him as he speaks, trying to force the sensitive, complex, private Ed out into the public sphere.

'Is that *true*, Ed?' I aped the tone of a primary school headmistress. '*Do* you think it's not all my fault?'

'You've got a persecution complex. You're a trouble-maker. You're determined to make life difficult for the whole family!'

'Ed!' Sally shrieked. 'He doesn't think that! He just refuses to say what's expected of him. He thinks it's undignified to say the "obvious right thing".' Sally drew quote marks in the air.

As the debate continued, and as Ed proceeded to fortify his dignity and misrepresent himself to an almost staggering degree, over and over again, I thought about all the things Sally had told me he'd said to Roberta, on occasions when I was not present: 'You've been chipping away at Jane for ever with your bitchy remarks, it's no wonder she doesn't trust you. You can't pretend you're the innocent victim this time. Grow up! Ring Jane and apologise.' Strangely, Ed is able to represent himself with startling accuracy in my absence. A less charitable person might have become suspicious by now, but I've decided, out of sisterly loyalty, to believe in the Ed Sally describes, the one who tirelessly battles away on my behalf. I wish she would reciprocate by believing in the Carl who's never stopped loving me and who is going to apologise at some point in the near future.

Carl. Nutshell: we had a fling, he said he loved me, I said I loved him (which was true, though I had no intention of leaving Dom. Perhaps the thing with

Carl was infatuation rather than love. I have never been able to resist strong-jawed, beefy men with rough skin and roots in the underclass.) Then one night Carl and I had dinner with his colleague Jason and Jason's girlfriend Dawn. The evening went well, and when Jason asked Carl's advice about the best route home, Carl told him to head north and follow signs for the motorway. I knew this wasn't the quickest way, so I said, 'No, it's better to go back through the town centre and get on to the motorway at junction twelve – it'll save you loads of time.' Jason seemed pleased.

As soon as we were alone, Carl turned on me with a face like a gargoyle. 'You fucking *bitch*!' he snarled. 'How dare you try to humiliate me in front of *my* friends! You have to have the last word, don't you? "No, it's better to go through the town centre. It'll save you loads of time." ' His impression of my voice was a high-pitched whine. Actually, I have quite a low voice for a woman. I hate to nit-pick, but once truth and accuracy are sacrificed, it's the slippery slope for all things prized and valuable.

'Carl, I was just . . .' I protested.

'I spent the first fucking twenty years of my life being told everything I did was wrong, and I'm not going to be made to feel that way again by a cocky bitch like *you*!' He stormed off, leaving me stranded, carless. I hitched a lift home, half hoping I'd be garrotted by a dysfunctional loner who still lived with his mother. Why hadn't I kept my big mouth shut? Why did I always have to butt in?

Nearly six months passed before I would allow Sally and the one or two friends of mine who knew about Carl to persuade me that suggesting a quicker way home was not so heinous a crime. I know they're right. I absolutely know it beyond any shadow of a doubt. It's just that I'd quite like Carl to realise it, and tell me he's realised. Does this explain why I nearly degraded myself by humming *Happy Birthday* while prodding my collarbone in public? I needed rationality from the most unreasonable man I've ever known. I saw no other way forward; Carl had to exonerate me.

'That's ridiculous,' Sally often said. 'He's unhinged. What does it matter what he thinks?'

'Look, a pardon's only worth something if it comes from the person who originally condemned you,' I tried to explain. 'I mean, how would the Birmingham Six or the Guildford Four have felt if they'd been acquitted by . . . Jamie Oliver instead of by a court of law? It wouldn't have carried the same weight, would it?'

After several hundred repeats of this conversation, Sally lost the will to say, 'That's different.' She simply shook her head and turned ever so slightly paler.

'And I can't just write Carl off as unhinged. I can't ignore the evidence that doesn't suit that hypothesis, and there's plenty.'

'Like what?'

'All the sane, sensible, true things he's said. His rational everyday persona. Why do you think I was so stunned when he turned on me? I'd never seen even a hint of irrationality before that night.'

'What sane, sensible, true things?' Sally rolled her eyes, like someone succumbing to a lethal injection.

'He said *The Crimson Petal and the White* is a brilliant book, and it is.'

'Oh, for God's sake!' It annoyed Sally when I misrepresented myself as a love-crazed fool who couldn't bring herself to think badly of the monster who broke her heart.

\*

A week after my argument with Ed about Roberta and Sally's argument with Ed about Ed, I went to Shrewsbury to talk about one of my documentaries at the annual film festival. In the foyer of the building where my event was taking place, I spotted my dad lurking near the book stall, wearing a green cagoule and a pair of bi-focals I hadn't seen before. Oh, God, I thought. What was he doing here, miles away from Taunton? My father is not very well, and does not leave the house, or leave town, unless it is absolutely necessary. Even before he got ill, he once took an aluminium blanket and a whistle with him on a day trip to Exeter, in case of an emergency.

In addition to his physical ailments, he'd been in a bad state emotionally since Roberta left him, and, while I'd written to him often and tried to say consolatory, supportive things, I had so far avoided seeing him. I didn't think I'd be able to resist saying something tactless like, 'So what if she left you for your doctor?' (It's a long story.) 'At least you're rid of the bony fucker!'

I didn't feel ready to face my dad yet, so I retreated to the festival speakers' green-room. Once inside, something significant happened to me, very quickly. I'd go so far as to say that the speed was inappropriate, given the significance; important things should happen slowly. Still, however transitory it was, I recall every second in precise detail. Is the precision something I've added retrospectively? Was it all a bit of a blur, while it was actually taking place? I don't think so. I'm too controlled and suspicious a person to partake of a blur, even briefly.

I met a young blonde woman who'd written a factual book about bees, which someone had turned into a film. We started to chat, though I was barely paying attention; my mind was still veering Dadwards.

The woman introduced me to her husband, David Soundy, and I recognised the name. It was an unusual one, but I'd heard Carl use it. 'That posh twat Soundy' had been his exact words. I was on the point of deciding that it had to be a coincidence when I heard the name of the production company for which Carl used to work. David Soundy was telling me that he worked there too. So did Bee Woman.

My pulse quickened. Out of the corner of my eye, I saw a rotund pensioner heading my way, wearing a white plastic festival staff badge. I knew she was here to take me to the auditorium, for sound checks and chair checks and lectern checks and all the other unnecessary checks event organisers like to inflict upon performers. I felt time leaking away, gushing out of a hole that grew bigger by the second. All those hours and days and months I'd spent agonising over Carl; all the thinking I'd done on the subject of our relationship – the deep and the frantic, the vengeful and the hopeful – it was preparation for this moment, this encounter with Bee Woman and David Soundy. This was the culmination. I had to do something, make it fruitful.

'You don't by any chance know Carl Larder, do you?' I asked.

Soundy shook his head.

'Only vaguely,' said Bee Woman. Instantly, she looked wary. 'I went to a couple of parties he was at. I knew *of* him.'

'What did you think of him, if you don't mind my asking?'

'Well . . .' She turned and looked over her shoulder, as if afraid Carl might leap out at any moment with a machete. 'Like I said, I didn't really know him, but . . . I always thought he seemed a bit weird.'

I wanted to kiss her. Here was independent corroboration of Sally's theory, from a non-partisan source. Suddenly, I was desperate for this blonde stranger to denigrate Carl. It didn't matter that she hadn't known him well. In fact, it was a bonus. She'd never been in love with him, therefore she was more capable of objectivity than I'd ever been. 'Weird how?' I asked casually, not wanting to prejudice her answer.

'Well . . . a bit violent.'

As she said it, something seemed to wash over me, or wash off me. I felt light and free, as if I'd just climbed out of an uncomfortable costume.

Hallelujah! Carl was officially weird and violent! My broken heart was entirely his fault, not mine! Everyone thought so! By now the round-shouldered festival assistant had reached me and was plucking at my sleeve. I squeezed the blonde woman's arm and said 'I have to go now, but thanks. You don't know how much you've helped me.'

She frowned, puzzled. I hope she concluded, after I'd gone, that Carl had once held me captive in a soundproof dungeon and tried to excise my eyeballs with a pocket knife, perhaps for contradicting his motoring advice. It wasn't too far from the truth.

My dad fell asleep in my lecture. Afterwards, he waited for me outside. 'Can we talk?' he said. 'It's quite important.'

'Sure.'

We found a café on the high street and sat down at a table by the window. Dad seemed nervous. I assumed he wanted to talk about Roberta. I knew it would be hard for him to admit he'd been wrong; hence his long silence. 'Why can't you make television programmes about nice things?' he said eventually. 'All that suffering and oppression. It's no wonder you're . . .'

'What? Perfectly cheerful?' And I was, thanks to Bee Woman. I felt weightless, euphoric, magnanimous. Unlike Dad, I was desperate to revel in how wrong I'd been. I was wrong, wrong, wrong to love Carl. 'I can't stomach injustice, Dad. That's what drives me. What sort of programmes would you like me to make?'

'Good old dramas. Like *Monarch of the Glen.*'

'I see. And you came all the way from Taunton to tell me this?'

He reddened. 'No. I'm afraid I'm here to talk about Roberta.'

'Ah.' Not that putrid slapper, I thought. 'Look, Dad, we all fall for grimsters once in a while. Love really is blind. The important thing is to . . .'

'Please don't call Roberta grim, Jane.'

'Hey?' Had Dad forgotten that, when he was first diagnosed with emphysema, Roberta and his GP Hugh Latham had bonded, in their mutual anguish and concern for his health, to such a great extent that they had started sleeping together?

'I'm here in heroic mode, on Roberta's behalf,' Dad said, resting his elbows on the table.

'*What?*'

'She's devastated that you don't want her to have a relationship with your children. She feels like their grandmother.'

'We..e..ell, she isn't,' I said flippantly. 'Mum is. Dom's mum is. Roberta's just a putrid old slapper.' It was too good a description to waste.

'I visited her the other day. She's got photos of them all over the flat.'

'How . . .?' I sighed. It had to be either Dad or Ed. 'I'm not even going to ask.'

'What does she need to do, Jane? All she wants is to be friends.'

'As I've made clear time and time again, what

she needs to do, in that case, is promise that she'll stop making snide remarks every time she sees me. And the subtle, non-verbal digs have got to go too, like pretending to forget my name. And pretending she thinks my birthday's the twenty-fifth of April when she knows damn well it's the nineteenth. That's all. It's very simple. For anybody who isn't a festering viper.'

'But you're the only person who thinks that, Jane.' Dad looked bewildered. I could hardly mention Sally's undercover dislike of Roberta. 'All her friends think she's the kindest, gentlest. . .'

'All my friends like me,' I said flatly. 'That doesn't prove anything. Dad, I don't get it. Roberta left you for your doctor, and claimed, with a straight if fossilised face, that the two of them were so sensitive to your plight and so traumatised by your being sick that they needed to turn to each other for support and consolation. As if *they* were the victims of your illness.' Rather than the beneficiaries, I thought but didn't add. Even someone as blunt as I am can be tactful. Ish.

'That wasn't why Roberta left me,' Dad insisted. 'She didn't leave me for Hugh.'

'Of course not. What was the official reason again? Oh, yeah: you never took the dog for a walk.'

'I exploited her.' Dad looked crestfallen. 'I left all the domestic labour to her. I took her for granted.'

'You loved her, Dad. I'm not denying that you're annoying to live with, but . . . everyone could see how much you adored Roberta.'

'Yes.' He looked encouraged. 'I *did*, didn't I?'

'You did. But you didn't do your share of the household chores, so she left you. Which, naturally, she'd have done even if Hugh and his dosh hadn't come along. It had absolutely nothing to do with him. It was all your fault.' Would Dad's love for Roberta dry up and fall away, like a dead verruca, if I blasted it with my sarcasm?

'I'm not denying that Roberta hurt me, but . . . I still like and trust her. You're so black and white.'

'And how do you feel about Hugh?'

My father snarled. 'I'll never speak to him again! I thought he was a decent man. If I ever got my hands on him, he'd be sorry . . .'

I nodded. 'Exactly. We're all black and white about what matters to us.'

'I never heard Roberta say anything horrible to you. Not once.'

'What a coincidence! Look, Dad, I think you'd get over this a lot more easily if, instead of thinking of Roberta as some great asset you've lost, you could start to think of her as a pestilent creep who hoodwinked you. Buy that CD by Eamon, *I Don't Want You Back*, the one that goes, "Fuck what I said, it don't mean shit now . . ." '

'I think you're a very dangerous and manipulative person,' he interrupted me.

'Dad, manipulative people operate covertly. Whereas I'm quite openly trying to turn you against Roberta. I suggest that you begin to loathe and deride her forthwith. You'll feel a lot better.' I couldn't, of course, tell him about weird, violent Carl, but I didn't see why what worked for me shouldn't work for him.

'I see there's no point in my even trying,' Dad said, looking glum. 'This was my last heroic act. Oh well!'

'You keep calling yourself heroic. Roberta won't change her mind, Dad, even if you secure a couple of grandchildren for her. She's got Hugh now, with his many properties. And let's not forget his rich mother who's yet to die and bequeath her diamonds to that special daughter-in-law . . .'

'Okay, Jane. Okay. Enough.'

I grunted and signalled for the bill. It came to ten pounds seventy-nine, which was a bit steep considering we'd only had a pot of tea for two. My father was aghast, but refused to query the amount and wouldn't allow me to do so. He hates to draw attention to himself. 'It's okay, I'll get it,' I said. 'I can claim it back on expenses.'

His face lit up. 'Really?'

Not really. The festival were paying me a fee for my talk, and travel expenses, but that was it. But it made me feel better to save Dad that five pounds and thirty-six pence. I knew how upset he was. He must have hated having to call me dangerous and manipulative. As a general rule, however, I don't plan to buy refreshments for everybody who besmirches my character; I'd be very poor very soon if I were to adopt that approach.

Sitting opposite my dad, I realised I could recover from Carl. Listening to Bee Woman was step one. Step two was recognising that not everyone in my situation would be capable of listening to their Bee Woman equivalent, or willing to do so. I was Dad's Bee Woman, and he was choosing to reject my help. His insistence that Roberta was basically good made me feel stronger, by comparison. He was resisting an obvious cure. Not like me; I was a survivor, a convert to sensible thinking. Bee Woman had spoken, and I Believed. I was confident that my heart would catch up with my head eventually. If I could meet a few more people who shuddered at the thought of Carl, that would definitely help.

What help was there for Dad? Roberta and Hugh were likely to outlive him, since neither of them had emphysema. At his funeral, they would sob all over everyone and say moistly that their love for Dad brought them together. They would be the most visibly grief-stricken people present, and absolutely nobody, not even me, would say 'How soon after the diagnosis did you two start shagging?'

It occurred to me that perhaps I wasn't the best person to make Dad see sense. Sally's attempts at rationality had, after all, been wasted on me; she was too close to the situation. Perhaps someone new and unknown was required, someone untarnished by past history.

'Dad?'

'Yes, dear?'

'Would you have any objection to my trying to fix you up with nice single middle-aged women? I know quite a few. Through work.'

His eyes darted left, then right. He cleared his throat and said, in the manner of someone accepting his first free rocks of crack cocaine from a predatory dealer – a freebie this time, to get him hooked – 'I don't suppose it'd do any harm. Yes, why not?'

# MARY SHARRATT
## Family Man

Will rocked on his heels in front of John William Waterhouse's painting, *La Belle Dame Sans Merci*. Its appearance in Manchester Art Gallery commemorated the ongoing Pre-Raphaelite Retrospective. Posters of that barefoot waif twining her hair like a noose around the armoured knight's neck had been plastered all over his hotel lobby.

Surrounded, as he was, by black-leather-jacketed Mancunians, Will wondered if his Hush Puppies and his sky-blue Goretex parka made it painfully obvious that he was American. Returning his attention to the painting, he tilted his head to see past the light reflecting on the dark surface. In his mind, the piece was overdone. The girl literally wore a heart stitched onto her sleeve. He moved to a portrait of a mermaid with blood-red hair. Clearly the artist had used the same model – a girl who looked no older than fifteen. In the next piece, *Hylas and the Nymphs*, a man crouched over a pool, mesmerised by naked girls rising like lotus flowers from the green rippling water. Disturbingly, the girls seemed to be predators and the hapless male onlooker their prey. Turning away, he headed for the gift shop to buy souvenirs for his wife and daughter.

This free afternoon felt like a fluke. He wasn't used to unstructured time. Most business trips were so tightly scheduled that he barely had a chance to poke his head out and breathe between rushing from his hotel to his scheduled appointments, but the morning's meetings had wrapped up early. His only further obligation was dinner with some associates that evening. After dropping the gifts for his family in his hotel room, Will armed himself with a tourist brochure and headed for Castlefield, which the pamphlet informed him was the cradle of the Industrial Revolution.

Three o'clock in the afternoon, it was already getting dark, grey sky deepening to the colour of a bruise. He paced cobbled streets threading through a tangle of early Victorian railway viaducts arching hundreds of feet above his head. Enclosing him on all sides were the hulking brick edifices of some of the world's oldest factories and industrial mills, which had been sandblasted and done over into café-bars and restaurants. He tried to imagine what this place must have looked like during its hey day. Once the turgid brown canal he walked along would have been an open sewer.

Heading away from the canal, he followed the pedestrian sign indicating the way to the Museum of Science and Industry, which the pamphlet assured him was a must-see. Music wafted out of a café-bar – some catchy tune from the Eighties that he had once loved, though he could no longer remember its name. As he racked his memory, a young woman appeared on the pavement ahead of him. Her mane of cloudy red hair was like nothing he had seen outside a painting. Her face was a Pre-Raphaelite portrait come to life, skin so white that she seemed to glow in the grainy winter dusk.

He was close enough to say hello, or ask directions to the museum, but before he could find the words, she ambled off and vanished behind one of the Gothic railway arches. At that moment, it started to rain. The cold and damp from the cobblestones seeped up his legs, making him shiver. He studied the map to find the most direct way to the museum.

Will found himself in an exhibit on the history of lavatories, ranging from Roman latrines to a spotlit display of Victorian toilets, some of them boasting lavish, hand-painted floral motifs, designed by the appropriately named Thomas J Crapper. An authentic length of Victorian sewer pipe, roughly twenty yards long, led to the next exhibit. He had to duck his head when he stepped inside. Happily, none of the original smells remained, just the dark corroded surface. What was it made of? He reached out to finger it, then his hand fell.

At the other end of the dark tunnel, a woman stood silhouetted by the bright light outside. Her face and body were in shadow, but her hair was a fiery nimbus. The young woman he had seen beneath the viaduct.

The sewer swallowed the noise of his footsteps as he stepped toward her. She cupped her hand to her mouth. Her thin shoulders bobbed up and down. When he reached the end of the tunnel, close enough to stretch out his hand and touch her, he saw that her face was streaked with tears. In her fist, she clutched a wadded-up tissue.

He spoke before he could stop himself. 'Are you okay, miss? Is there something wrong?' The sound of his own incongruous American accent jarred as it bounced off the curving sewer walls.

Her eyes were the colour of the sea. The blood rushed from her neck to her hairline, as though he had caught her in some forbidden act. He couldn't say how long she stared at him like that. Her lips moved, as if poised to say something. Abruptly she spun away, her hair swishing out in an arc that touched his face. A long moment passed before he could move again. He breathed with difficulty. He could not explain why he felt as though he had just taken a blow to the gut.

Just past nine o'clock that evening, Will sat in a pub with his colleague Dave and with Simon and the rest of the middle-management team from UK headquarters. The scarred wooden table was littered with pint glasses, overflowing ashtrays, and dinner plates that the staff had not yet bothered to clear away. The fish curry Will had consumed took uneasy residence inside his stomach. He had also imbibed far more alcohol than he would have normally considered feasible. His companions kept ordering more rounds. Now they were talking about going to a nightclub, no matter that tomorrow was a working day.

'I don't think so,' Will heard himself say. 'I don't want to be hung over for my flight tomorrow.' As if he wouldn't be hung over as it was. 'Think I'll just head back to the hotel and catch an early night.'

By the time they finally spilled out of the pub, Will was already feeling a bit more sober.

'Taxis are around the corner.' Simon led the way.

Will glanced around, trying to decide if the city looked less gloomy by night. Then he saw her, standing beneath the street lamp, except this time that cloud of red hair was piled on top of her head. She was wearing enough make-up for an entire theatrical company. Her mouth was a scarlet gash. She tottered unsteadily on stiletto heels. Her peacock-blue minidress exploded in the dull sodium light. She wore no coat or nylons; her legs were as bare as her arms in the December chill. At first he tried to persuade himself that he was mistaken. How could this be the same girl he had seen in the museum? That make-up, that obscenely short dress, the way she stood on the street corner, positioned to advertise herself to every passing car. There was no mistaking what she was.

Dave nudged his arm. 'Check *her* out.'

She locked eyes with Will. Recognition blazed on her face. Will couldn't look away from her, even as Simon and the others turned the corner.

'Are you coming?' Dave gave his sleeve a tug.

A bullet-headed man with a shaved scalp wrapped his fist around the girl's slender arm and barked at her – something in the local dialect that Will couldn't make out.

'C'mon,' said Dave. 'They're waiting for us.'

Will winced at the way the man seized her bare arm hard enough to bruise. Those stiletto heels looked like they were about to break her feet, yet she moved surprisingly fast. Before Will could exhale, she hobbled over to him and twined her fingers around his arm. When she lifted her face to his, he could see she had been crying, but was trying to mask it with a broad smile.

'Looking for a good time, sir?' Her eyes were full of silent pleading.

The bullet-headed man lurched toward them. Will felt his legs turn to mush.

In the background, he heard Dave calling, 'Just walk away from them, Will. Don't get involved.'

The girl clung to Will and bowed her head, cowering, as the bullet-headed man closed in.

'Take it easy,' Will heard himself say. 'Back off. You're frightening the young lady.' His accent seemed to work as a charm. The bullet-headed man hesitated and, at that moment, Will took the girl's hand and sprinted around the corner to the taxi queue. Pulling the girl behind him, he dived into a hackney cab and slammed the door behind them. He looked at the girl's flushed, downcast face.

'Tell him', he said with a nod to the Asian driver, 'where you want to go.' Will was sweating, breathless. Through the window, he could see the bullet-headed man watching. Dave looked on in disbelief.

The girl's knees were trembling, but she leaned forward and blurted an address that meant nothing to Will. The driver nodded and took off. Meeting Will's eyes in the rear-view mirror, he winked.

Will retreated to his corner, at least a foot away from the girl, who sat primly, legs and arms crossed, as though willing herself to take up as little space as possible. A voice at the back of Will's head said that none of this was really happening. He had always stayed far away from trouble. So clean cut that even his wife told him he was boring. Too conventional. He wondered how he would explain it to Dave the following day. He tried to convince himself that Dave was so drunk, he would only have the haziest memory of this night.

During the rest of the drive, Will stared out of the window at the dilapidated buildings they passed. A derelict cinema covered in graffiti. A crumbling old church bore a sign that read Caribbean Glow Tanning and Nail Bar. A high-rise, Sixties era apartment block had been abandoned, its upper windows glassless and empty, its lower windows and doors boarded up. Why did they just let it stand there like that, a crack den in the making, instead of tearing it down?

The driver turned off the main road and onto a smaller street with a string of shabby shops and pubs, half of them vacant and up for sale. A pile of building rubble and abandoned mattresses filled an empty lot. They drove under railway viaducts, past factories that looked as though they hadn't been used in fifty years. There was a row of terraced houses, televisions casting unearthly blue light behind net curtains. Coming to a dead end, the taxi pulled up in front of a hideous tenement.

While Will fished the fare from his wallet, the girl wriggled out of the car.

'Keep the change.' Will realised he was overtipping, but this didn't seem the right moment to be anal about such things.

The driver smiled in what resembled a kind of roguish compassion. 'Want me to wait for you, mate?'

Will felt himself blush. Out of the corner of his eye, he saw the girl standing near the tenement door.

'Might be difficult', said the driver, 'trying to find another car when you're ready to go home.'

'It's not what you think. I just want to make sure she'll be okay.'

Did he imagine it, or did the driver laugh under his breath? The most sensible thing would be to jump straight into that taxi and head for the hotel. He'd probably be back hours earlier than Dave. But would it be right to leave her like this? He thought of the way her knees had shaken in the car. He had seen real fear in her eyes.

'Just wait here for a minute,' Will told the driver.

The girl stabbed her key into the lock and opened the peeling, graffiti-stained door. Harsh fluorescent light poured out around her while she stood on the threshold.

He stepped toward her. 'Are you going to be all right?'

'I . . .' She spoke in a tight, scared voice. 'I don't fancy standing out here for long, if you know what I mean. Could you please ask the driver to go? He's drawing attention to the place.'

It came together in Will's head. Bullet Head was obviously her pimp. He had seen her leave with Will and might try to track her down. A taxi waiting outside her building would indicate that she was doing business. Bullet-Head would be able to keep score. But if Will waved the taxi off, how would he get back to the hotel?

The girl raised her face to his. 'Please.' Her breath caressed his cheek. When had a woman ever looked at him the way she did now?

Reaching into his coat pocket, his fingers located his cell phone. He would call for another cab. 'Okay,' he said, signalling the driver to leave.

It seemed that he could not step inside that door fast enough. Her hands shook as she locked it behind them.

'My place is at the top,' she said. 'Sorry there's no lift.'

He could barely hear her over the trill of high-pitched Indian music – some woman wailing in a language he couldn't understand. The music competed with TV gunshots and screams.

Staggering on stiletto heels, she led him up four flights of creaking wooden stairs. When he found his eyes resting on her bare white legs, he made himself look instead at the dirty green wallpaper, which depicted shepherdesses in low-cut dresses. Someone had taken a magic marker and scrawled initials and pictures of huge pricks. By the time they reached her door at the top landing, he was breathing hard.

While she struggled with four different locks, he noticed a scar beside her door. The wallpaper was torn and plaster spilled out. It looked as though someone had rammed an axe into the wall. Will tried to swallow, but there was no saliva left in his throat. What if this was some scam? For all he knew, there was another pimp in there waiting to beat him up, strip him of his cash and credit cards. Why had he let the driver leave without him?

The girl finally managed to open the door. Entering the dark space, she groped around until she found the switch to a low lamp, its shade swathed in a diaphanous blue-green shawl. Dim ocean-coloured light revealed paintings of undulating mermaids that covered the walls. There were even mermaids on the low slanting ceiling.

'Please come in.' There was an urgent undertone in her voice. After he had done so, she secured all four locks.

He glanced around the room. There was a bed covered with a spread of sea-green cotton. A folding table and two mismatched chairs. A shoe box-sized fridge, tiny wash-basin and kettle. A half-open closet door revealed a tangle of clothing and what looked to be a laundry bag. Nothing sinister, he told himself.

The girl kicked off her high heels and put on a pair of flat slippers.

'Would you like a brew then?' Her voice was full of anxious solicitude.

'A brew?' He watched her fill the kettle from the wash-basin tap.

'Tea,' she translated.

'Yes. Why not?' He tried to smile. At least the blue-green light made her make-up appear less garish. She pulled out a chair for him.

'Thanks ever so much,' she said, her back to him as she plucked tea bags out of a tin canister and plonked them into two mugs. 'You helped me out back there.'

'Who was that man?' Will watched a shiver travel down her back. Her palm clutched the place on her arm where Bullet-Head had grabbed her.

'Kevin,' she said in a dull voice.

'You work for him?'

'Used to,' she said. 'First off, I were in debt. But I'm on me own now. He still thinks I owe him, though.'

'Can you do anything about it?' Will asked. 'Go to the police?'

She laughed. The kettle whistled.

'I don't even know your name.' Will watched her pour boiling water into the mugs.

'Angel. And yours?'

'Will.'

'Do you take milk or sugar in your tea, Will?'

'Just sugar, please.'

She tore open a paper sugar packet, probably swiped from some café. Angel couldn't be her real name, he thought. But even if it was only her professional handle, it struck him as an odd choice. He found himself staring at her with the wonder of a teenage boy. Her long legs, slim back, the nape of her neck, her pile of hair which he ached to touch. Biting his lip, he reminded himself that this girl wasn't much older than his daughter.

'What part of America are you from?'

He wondered why she should be so curious, then told himself to stop being so paranoid. This was just small talk, the kind you would expect from any cab driver or waitress. 'Minnesota.'

'Is it nice country?' She pronounced the word *coon-tray*.

'I suppose. Although I don't get out to the countryside very often.'

She handed him a mug with a picture of a sheep on it and the caption *I love ewe*.

The sweet scalding tea braced him for what he had to say next. 'Look, I only came up here to see if you were going to be okay. The way you approached me tonight. Well, it sure looked like you needed rescuing.'

She sat in the other chair, hands cupping her mug. Its handle had broken off. 'Thanks again. It were good of you to take me into your taxi.'

'There's not a whole lot else I can do,' said Will. 'I'm flying home tomorrow. Are you going to be all right? Are you safe here?' He glanced at the four bolts on the door.

'Safe as I'll ever be. Didn't expect to run into Kevin tonight.' She sipped from her mug.

'Is there anyone you can turn to if you need help?' he asked. 'Your family? How old are you, anyway?'

'Eighteen,' she replied, a bit too defensively. A bitter look crossed her face. 'Not much in the way of family. When me parents died, me and me sisters went into care. Split us up and put us into different homes, they did. The authorities never know what to do with orphaned families what haven't any money.' Then she bowed her head and went on in a softer voice. 'Learned to take care of me-self. I do all right.'

Will recalled the horror stories he had heard about children who were raised in foster care. Maybe she had run away, ended up on the street where she had fallen victim to the pimps and pushers. 'As long as Kevin leaves you alone.'

'It's a way to earn a bit of money is all.' She spoke with dignity. 'But it's not all I am.' She held him with her blue-green eyes.

'What are you really?'

Even in the dim light and under the thick coat of make-up, he saw the blood rise under her pale skin. She said nothing.

Will rolled his head back to look at the mermaids on the ceiling. 'Did you do these?'

'Every one.'

The paintings were well rendered, he thought.

She was certainly talented.

'You belong at art school,' he said.

She took his remark in her stride. 'I'll get there one day.'

Will drained his tea while Angel went on sipping hers. He could think of nothing more to say. In the silence, he couldn't keep himself from looking at her. He wished she would wipe off that make-up so he could see her true face as he had in the museum. Yet even with the make-up and horrible hair-do, she was the most beautiful young woman.

As though reading his mind, she glanced at him and set her mug aside. 'Would you be wanting anything then, Will?' Her lips curved. 'Any services?'

The way she looked at him. He was gripped by the strongest lust he had known in years. A voice inside him told him to just do it. Dave and the others had seen him getting into the taxi with her. Everyone would assume that was what he had done. He might as well live up to his damaged reputation.

'I'm married,' he said, as if that would make any difference to Angel. Probably most of her clients were married. What did she care?

'You have a family, then.'

'A wife and a daughter. She's sixteen.'

Angel smiled, revealing long crooked teeth. 'Family man.'

She reached out and stroked his thigh. He didn't push her hand away. But even as his desire flared, he discovered he was very tired. The jet lag was catching up with him, not to mention the pints he had downed at the pub. His weariness was overpowering. A black tide filled his head, a rip tide dragging him under.

Will awoke in the dull grey light coming through the dormer window. In a panic, he sat up, then looked at his watch, which had stopped at 12:55 am. Angel was gone.

Scrambling for his shoes, he noticed a plastic clock on the window-sill. It was 8:45. His plane left at 10:30. He still needed to go back to the hotel and collect his luggage, then get himself to the airport. Why had she let him oversleep? And where had she gone?

Christ, this room was ugly. By the dim lamplight, it had taken on a certain quirky charm, but by the light of day, it was appalling. The flocked beige wallpaper, over which the mermaids had been painted, was speckled with mildew. Outside the unwashed window, rain lashed down. He heard it drum on the roof, saw rust-coloured water stains on the ceiling between the mermaids, who now resembled drowned women. Ghosts. He thought he, too, was drowning.

Then he saw his wallet splayed open in the middle of the floor. He grabbed it, frantically fingering the cash and credit cards, all intact. But when he reached into his pocket for his cell phone, he discovered it was gone.

The ewe on the empty mug grinned. He remembered the way Angel had prepared the tea, her back to him. She had drugged him, slipped something into his mug. Doped him and stolen his mobile, slipped his wallet out of his pocket. But why leave the wallet behind? Something must have distracted her. Something must have interrupted her before she could finish the job. Maybe the pimp was planning to come and beat him. He had to get out.

At the door, he panicked, wondering if he would be able to undo the four locks. Gripping the doorknob, he twisted and pushed. The door opened freely.

As he sprinted down the stairs, a veiled Muslim woman came in the main door and began climbing the steps. Since the staircase was so narrow, he was forced to make eye contact with her as he squeezed past. The look she gave him could have scraped paint off a brand-new car. She glared at him as though he were dirt, as though she could see and smell the corruption on him. As though she had a very good idea why he was creeping down the stairs, dishevelled and uncombed at this hour. Glancing away, he stumbled and had to grab the railing to keep himself from falling.

Will only made his plane because it was delayed two hours owing to weather conditions. He put his hand luggage containing the gifts for Liz and Emma in the overhead compartment before settling into his aisle seat. Dave, already ensconced in the adjoining window seat, was nursing his hangover with airline champagne. He raised his glass.

'Cheers to you, buddy. I didn't know you had it in you.'

Before Will could reply, the flight attendant held out a tray of champagne and orange juice. Will chose the juice.

'Quite a looker,' Dave continued. 'Seemed awfully young, though. Sure she was legal?'

'She set me up.' Will looked directly into Dave's bloodshot eyes to prove that he had nothing to hide. 'I thought she was in trouble. I wanted to make sure she got home safely . . .'

Dave cut him off. 'Man, anyone watching could tell that was a set-up. So why did you stay out *all night*? For your information, I was worried about you. Knocked on your door this morning, had housekeeping open it, and your bed hadn't been slept in. I was wondering if I needed to call the police and file a missing person report. I was asking myself what

I would have to tell your wife.'

Will wanted to belt him. He fastened his seat belt instead. 'It was a set-up,' he repeated. 'I think she drugged me.' He told Dave about the tea.

Dave's face softened. 'That's creepy. You report it to the police?'

'No. I just want to put it behind me.' A trickle of sweat ran down his spine. 'Let's keep this between us, okay?'

When the safety demonstration began, Will leaned back, closed his eyes, breathed deeply, tried to force himself to relax. Everything, he told himself, was back to normal. He leafed through the in-flight magazine. There was an article about Swiss ski resorts. A photograph showed a happy family unit about to take off down a pristine white slope.

Nothing happened. He hadn't sinned, had only done what he thought was right, helping out a lost soul. Or had he? Would he have stepped in and done the same thing for a less beautiful girl? *Stop torturing yourself. You didn't even touch her.* That wasn't strictly true. He had taken her hand when making the lunge for the taxi. But it had been a completely chaste encounter and it was over. In eight hours, he would be home. Liz would pick him up at the airport. After four days' absence, she would be glad to see him. Maybe they would make love.

Emma would come out of her room with that sleepy, blinking expression of hers and ask him about Manchester. He would give her the poster he had bought for her.

He skimmed the article about Swiss family vacations. Perhaps he could take Liz and Emma to a bed and breakfast one weekend. They could go cross-country skiing. Severed from her computer for two entire days, Emma would learn to enjoy the outdoors,

77

get some colour in her face. Late at night, he and Liz could lounge in front of an open fireplace with a bottle of good wine.

Will took out his wallet to look at his family photos. They were gone.

The panic started in his bowels and travelled up his solar plexus, reaching his throat. Angel had taken them. Taken his pictures, not his money. The clear plastic accordion compartment with his family snapshots. He knew them by heart. Emma's baby picture and her most recent school picture. The snapshot of Liz, aged twenty-six and pre-Emma, in a white string bikini. A picture of him with his arms around Liz, back when he still had long hair. The family portrait taken last Christmas. Emma's unicorn picture, done in crayon and marker when she was in grade school and young enough to show her pictures off proudly and not hide them from sight. If she knew her father had kept one of them, she would probably die.

His family photos, Emma's unicorn – he would never get them back. In the place where the photo compartment had fit into his wallet, she had left a message scrawled on one of his business cards.

What a precious daughter you have. What a lovely wife. What would they do if they knew?

Their family Christmas portrait had their names, address and phone number on the back. She had his mobile with his home number on speed dial. For all he knew, she could be phoning right now. Liz and Emma would just be finishing breakfast, about to leave for work and school. His wife or daughter would grab the phone, thinking it was him, only to have a foreign hooker on the other end. A foreign hooker who knew their names.

But why? Why would anyone want to do this to him? The jagged-toothed smile she had given him when she called him family man. He imagined Angel's long red hair winding around his neck, choking him.

The plane hit turbulence, lurched violently, and the *Fasten Seat Belt* signs blinked on.

# LIZ KIRBY

## Lambswool

See, see! The first fat tear is forming at the corner of her eye. It trembles there. Her pearly white teeth bite into her lower lip and the shiny gloss that she favours smudges. She is trying to hold back. Oh don't restrain yourself my dear. Don't deny me the gift of your weeping. She twitches. Gives a little sniff and gulps. Still the ripe tear hangs in the balance. She blinks. Oh the joy! Her long lashes, heavy with thick mascara, sweep up and down. The movement tips the trembling tear down into the hollow below her eye, and it begins to make a slow track down her cheek. Delicious!

My tongue snakes out of its own accord, and I catch it on the tip just before it slips into the crevice at the side of her nose. It melts down my throat and expands like morning light inside me. It is a ripe rain of rich juice that will feed me for weeks. I breathe out my bliss against her soft neck and look straight into those dark wet eyes. Oh dear. The moment of romance is gone. She is truly weeping now. Big, wet, snivelling tears tumbling down. She should have worn waterproof mascara. Doesn't she have a tissue on her? She wipes the back of her hand under her nose and the slimy mess is smeared across her lower lip. The best is gone. I melt back into the shadows at the corner of the room and watch with interest to see what will happen next.

She sobs for several minutes. Really I am quite impressed. I wouldn't have thought she would go on for so long. Finally she finds the box of tissues that was in front of her, beside the bed, and blows her nose noisily. Thank goodness for that, it was becoming a bit disgusting. Her nose is red and her face blotched with smudged make-up. She is the prettier for it I would say. I often wanted to take a towel and wipe the paste off her young skin. She rubs her face and then curses gently seeing the black smear on the tissue, folds it over and begins to dab carefully under her lashes. She is very sweet don't you think? I took to her the moment I saw her in that smart little coat. She came in rosy faced from the early morning frost with her red scarf wrapped around her head and I thought, 'there's my girl' as I lay there, 'oh yes, there's my girl. In her red hood. She will bring him to me, if I am patient. I must just be patient.'

She has composed herself a little now and gone out to fetch the others. Soon they'll be busy with all their little tasks. Whatever they do to clean up and make a presentable façade out of the mess. The room is quiet and now I have a moment to consider the tough old flesh that lies there. Her sagging loose skin has turned a waxy yellow, and her eyes a blank watery blue. One breast flops out of the unbuttoned, brushed nylon nightdress, and the nipple has turned blue. Here they come with their bowls of disinfectant and their white plastic aprons. They whisk the flowered curtains round the bed, strip off the pale blue garment and begin to wash. My little sweet one still sniffing, the older one silently and briskly getting on with an extra job in a busy day. They lather and rinse the cold lumpen flesh, just as they did when it was alive, cleaning off the piss and shit, even combing the ragged strands of white hair.

The young one is quite tender and talks as she does it. 'Come on now Grandma, lift your arm up, I just need to wash under here. There's a good girl.' She pauses and sniffs again. 'Why didn't you tell me you were going to go? I would have liked the chance to say goodbye. I'd even made some cakes. Well I made them for my boyfriend, but I brought some here for you too. Lemon buns. You like them don't you?'

'You're too soft,' the older one butts in. 'You'll have to get used to it you know. They're old, they peg out all the time.' That makes her cry harder and for a moment I am angry. There is no need to upset her. But it is true isn't it? Of course I found a way out. But the others. They die all the time, all of them, demented and drivelling their way to silence. It was the sight of them that made me so determined.

I had enjoyed the peace and quiet at first. My old-lady phase, settling down and allowing my dinners to be brought to me, and my shopping delivered to the door. I didn't think there was any urgency, so I drifted, after so many hard years, into a pleasant dream. The days passed, long and lazy, and the heat dissolved my thoughts into a humid fog. It was summer and I was running in the woods, leaping over logs, slinking between the birch trees and drinking dark peaty water. Through my yellow eyes I saw the rabbit tails flashing in the dusk. My mouth watered and the saliva dripped from my teeth as I crouched. I could feel the crack of bone and the savoury squeal of a tender death. The saliva dripping. My eyes opened. Still dripping. My mouth twisted and my whole body inert. Had I cracked my own spine? When they finally broke the door down all I could do was glare at them as my face convulsed and my hands and legs twitched.

They all talked to me. 'Come on then Gran. I need to wash down below. Don't look at me like that now. You want to be clean now don't you? It's my job. I'll get into trouble if you get sores where your skin isn't clean.' My silence was taken as consent, and my white hair mistaken for gentleness. I snarled and growled through a slack mouth and they spooned baby food down my throat. At night I lay still on that narrow white bed, and stared up at the ceiling, trying to sense if the moon had risen. Listening for clues. Then Rosie walked down the corridor and into the ward. I watched her, thinking of the forest path, and she saw me, walked over and said, 'do you like my red scarf? It's lambswool. I just got it from Dotty P. Here.' And she wrapped it around my chilled hands as they lay crossed on my stomach. They had put them like that, when I was last turned. They do it every four hours. 'Can't have you getting bedsores. It's a sign of bad nursing.'

Then I began to track her. In the daytime they would tilt the head of the bed, so that I was propped up. I could watch then, every movement. She was light and lithe. Newly qualified and full of enthusiasm. She brought flowers into the room. Little posies that she filched from the 'less sentient ladies'. She sang as she worked, and talked to us all the time in a singsong voice, calling us all 'Gran' and chatting carelessly. I am not sure she knew when she wandered off the path, and became lost in the tangled undergrowth. She just kept nattering away and humming her infernally repetitive pop songs. 'I should be so lucky, lucky, lucky, lucky.' And the shadow followed her, quietly and persistently. It was drawn to her brightness. I knew it was there, watching and waiting for its moment. When she sat at the night desk and slept, I would call out, and the shadow would answer, from a long way off. The sound echoed through the valley and far-off voices caught its dying fall.

I put all my energies then to calling it closer. At first I would just see it as a flicker or a movement. But then one night they turned me onto my side and then forgot me for hours. I lay there staring at the one edge of the doorpost that I could see in the dim light. Two slanting oval eyes seemed to glow briefly in the dark. When I looked again they were gone. I wasn't sure. Was it a trick of the dark, or was something there? I waited. Breathing steadily and quietly. Yes, there it was again, a gleam of eyes, there and gone. He came so close, and then disappeared again. I had to bide my time, but the next time he was a little closer. Sitting at the foot of my bed. I couldn't see him but I could feel the warmth of his silent, watchful presence. I waited, patiently, in my helpless-old-lady body. Limp and damp with sweat. Each night it was the same. I whispered to him of the brightness of her face, the lilt of her voice. He crept up on me, silently to listen. A little closer each time. And I lay in a half world, sensing the gleam of his eyes, the soft touch of his coat and the lithe muscles beneath. Then the night came when I felt his breath on my cheek.

The warm moist air touched my face bringing me the stench of rancid meat and saliva. I breathed in sharply. Once. Twice. Three times. And leapt. My nails were long and sharp. The silly little girls were too lazy to cut them. I wanted to howl with laughter when I heard his yelp of dismay. I ripped his belly open in one tearing movement. Ahhh he was soft and lush inside. First my hand and then my arms slipped into the slit, as easily as slipping on a silk petticoat. One leg and then the other, wriggling and turning my head into its new casing. It was the work of a moment to force him out and take possession. A glorious new body of shadow and movement. Fit for the chase, fit for the hunt. The stupid creature was pawing and scrabbling. Trying to crawl his way back in. I crushed him with my strong new jaws, enjoying the crunch and rip as they met and tore. He had thought he was hunting me, but my instincts were finer and my cunning greater.

And now here I am, watching them turn the carcass on the bed, and lay a clean sheet over it. The snivelling one turns away first. She had a name. What was it? The plump, older one follows and they go to make a cup of tea. The shape on the bed glimmers white. A discarded sack, flaccid and shapeless. I twist my new slim body and flow from the dark corner of the room down the dim corridor, seeking the scent of wet leaves and hot animal fear, leaving the dead grandmother and the idiot granddaughter to comfort each other. I won't forget her. She brought me the wolf. And her tears were so delicious.

# SHERRY ASHWORTH

## Mimi

Jean entered the hallway of the terraced council house, circumvented the stroller in her path, and was led into a square, bare living room with a television murmuring in one corner, a paisley settee against one wall and, next to it, a cardboard box.

'She's the last one,' the woman said. 'The two boys went as a pair, and the other girl was taken yesterday.'

'That's okay,' Jean said. 'It doesn't matter.' She looked into the box. The mother cat was stretched out in a pose of deliberate inelegance, her belly exposed for all to see, saying, look what they've done to me. Those blasted kittens.

And there by her side, not feeding now, a black-and-white, murderous-looking, tiny, scraggy cat with poppy eyes, all skin and bones.

Jean said, 'Oh! She's very pretty!'

The kitten stared at her, disbelieving.

'She'll need her injections,' said the woman. 'What with four of them I couldn't. . .'

'No, no, of course. It's no trouble.'

Jean gazed at the kitten. It was quite ugly. The black and white was unevenly distributed – there were black blotches on its white face. Its ears were far too big for its body and stuck up like sails on a boat. It quivered. The smell that came from the box was not entirely pleasant. Jean thought, 'I really ought to walk right out of here. This is madness. As if I haven't got enough on my plate.'

'I'll take it,' she said.

'Now?' asked the woman.

'Yes – why not?'

The woman picked up the kitten and handed it to Jean. She could feel the tautness of the body and the surprising silkiness of its fur.

'I'll be glad to see the back of them, to be honest,' the woman said. 'Exploring everywhere. Hiding. Getting up to all sorts. And I suppose I'll have to get Maisie spayed but it costs so much.'

'Here,' said Jean. She handed the woman back the kitten while she opened her handbag, got out her purse and found some notes to give to the woman. 'That'll help.'

The woman was embarrassingly grateful. Jean took the kitten out into the hall.

'Have you got a cat carrier?' the woman asked.

'No. It's all right.'

Jean left, holding the kitten tight to her chest. She got into her car and placed the animal on the seat next to her.

'We're going home,' she said.

*

It was a moment of madness. She had seen the advertisement in the newsagent's window – kittens, free to good home, and thought, it would be nice to have a kitten. She mentioned at work that she was thinking about getting one. Doreen had said it would be good for her to have a cat; it would be a companion. Now that the kids had grown up. Now that she was getting older. A cat'll come and sit on your lap, keep you warm. Anne disagreed. 'They ruin your furniture,' she'd said. 'It's quite a responsibility, Jean, being a cat owner. You've never had a cat before, have you?'

Nor any other type of pet. The children had

demanded one when they were younger, but Ken had put his foot down. Too expensive. There was pet food and visits to the vet and kennels or catteries and what if it got ill? What if it died? Because they do die; they have shorter life spans than people. And the children won't get over it. But the real problem was Jean's mother.

The kitten didn't seem to mind being driven in the car. It put its front paws up to the window and stared out, its enormous ears like radar dishes primed to catch the slightest sound over the hum of the engine. Then it squirmed between the car seats to explore the back. Jean could see it in the mirror, perched by the rear window. Bored after a time, it came back and found its way to her lap. She hoped it wasn't going to get between the pedals and her feet. Keeping one hand on the steering wheel, with the other she stroked the little thing. It purred immediately. Jean filled with joy.

No one was home. Jean brought the kitten into the kitchen, where, earlier, she'd prepared a cat basket and placed a scratching post next to it, a cylinder like a mill chimney covered in rope, but with two plastic balls attached. The kitten ignored it, ignored the basket and instead ran quickly around the room, sniffing at everything. Jean watched it. It sniffed the skirting board, it burrowed into the corner by the vegetable rack, smelt the vegetables, leapt up onto the work surface, casing the joint, looking like a fugitive and detective rolled into one. Such a thin little thing. Jean wondered if it had been the runt of the litter. Maybe it had been undernourished. You could almost snap it in two.

On that thought Jean took out the tin of Whiskas kitten food from the cupboard and opened it. The kitten bounded across the work surface to investigate. As Jean forked it out onto the brand-new red plastic dish, the kitten nosed it and picked at it, with a determined daintiness.

'It's starving, the poor thing!' Jean thought to herself, and had that familiar satisfaction she got when people ate the food she'd provided. 'So thin, though. So thin.' She didn't think to put the dish down onto the floor, but watched the kitten eat in front of her.

'I shall call her Mimi,' Jean suddenly decided. 'Mimi. It suits her.'

\*

'Oh! Oh! How cute is she!' screamed Chrissie, Jean's teenage daughter. 'Can I pick her up? Oh look, she wants to get down already. Can I bring Shaz and Gabi and Laura round to see her? She is sooo gorge! What are we going to call her? I know – Rachel – like off *Friends*. Come here, Rachel. You pretty little – ow! She's got sharp claws. But what will Grandma do?'

'I'll keep her in the back bedroom when Grandma comes. And her name's Mimi.'

'No it isn't, it's Rachel. I'm going to call her Rachel. Rachy-Pachy!'

'You can play with her while I get on with dinner,' Jean said.

'Oh, I shan't be wanting dinner. Didn't I tell you I'm going round Shaz's? She's coming back here and staying over. Can you get the spare bed ready? Oh, and I need money for school tomorrow for the theatre trip. God, I'm knackered. I'm just gonna watch telly for a bit before I have a shower. Can I take Rachel in the front room with me?'

'Don't force her. Leave the door open and see if she'll follow you.'

When Ken got home from work he was a little reticent. He watched the kitten jab at the screwed-up piece of newspaper that Jean dangled at it from the end of a thread.

'She's a bit of a livewire,' he said.

'She'll calm down as she gets older,' Jean assured him.

'Hmm. She'll be a responsibility. I've been looking into a pet insurance plan. Just in case the worst happens. And have you thought what we'll do when we're on holiday? Once I retire – and that's only five years off, I'm hoping to get away quite a bit. We'll be having weeks in the country. And those Saga holidays are very reasonable, and we'll get to mix with like-minded people. Not those young people who get drunk and get up to mischief. We'll be away from all of that. Did I tell you, *The Great Escape*'s on telly tonight? Our favourite. Are you going to tell your mother about that cat?'

'I'll see.'

*

Luckily her mother rang to announce she'd be round so Jean had a chance to take Mimi, her basket, her toys and her litter tray up to the spare bedroom. It had been Chrissie's room until she took over Damon's when he went to college. There were still posters on the walls of various pop stars. Jean arranged everything so the kitten would be comfortable. Mimi liked the edge of the mat and kept pouncing on it. She had so much energy. Reluctantly Jean left her there, shutting the door softly. Before too long she heard her mother's ring at the door. She let her in.

Audrey was sprightly for her age. Despite her corrugated skin and iron-grey hair she was upright, neat and completely in control of her faculties. She unbuttoned her coat, folded it neatly and laid it across the banister.

'I thought I'd pop in and see how you are. I'm on my way to church, actually. The flower committee are meeting to discuss the arrangements for Easter. Did you try that sausage casserole recipe I cut out for you from *The People's Friend*? Too many onions, I thought. How's Ken? And Chrissie? She needs a bit of reining in, that girl, if you ask me. Out all hours. When you were her age, you were as good as gold. Never had any trouble with you, Jean. Ken was your first serious beau, wasn't he? And you were married at twenty-three. You always knew how to behave – no drinking, no fooling around. You were the sensible one.'

'I know, Mum.'

'Well, don't just stand there. Put the kettle on.'

They took their tea into the living room. Jean sipped hers thoughtfully. Ought she to say something about Mimi? But why risk a confrontation? Audrey was getting on for eighty. She was strong, but she didn't want to raise her blood pressure. And what the eye doesn't know . . .

'Your father's easy chair looks well by the curtains,' Audrey mused. 'It's quite an antique now. I'm glad I let you have it.'

'Yes, thanks, Mum.'

'Hmm.' Audrey lifted her cup to her mouth. Her eyes scanned the room, looking for something else to make conversation with. She noticed the door was ajar and was just about to comment that there was a bit of a draught when the colour drained from her face. Her hand shook uncontrollably. Tea splashed onto her lap. She went white, then red as she emitted a strangled scream. Jean followed her eyes to the door.

There was a little black-and-white face peeping round, eyes wide with curiosity.

'A cat! It's a cat! Jean, it's a cat! Get it out of here!'

Jean ran to the door, but it was too late. Mimi dived into the room and darted from corner to corner. Audrey had begun to hyperventilate. Beads of perspiration bedaubed her brow.

'Help! Where did it come from? Keep it away from me!'

'Go into the kitchen, Mum!'

After quite a few tries, Jean managed to seize Mimi. The kitten was red-hot with excitement. Jean buried her face in its pulsating little body. 'You silly thing,' she muttered. 'Didn't I tell you that my mother's terrified of cats? It's a proper phobia!'

*

Both Roger, Jean's older brother, and Kay, her sister, were incensed.

'You *know* Mum's feelings about cats. If you wanted a pet, you could have got a goldfish. And you didn't even warn her.'

'I'm sorry,' Jean had said. 'I'm sorry.'

'If you took it to the animal rescue I'm sure they could find a good home for it.'

'I suppose they could.'

Mimi was filling out. The skin that hung loose from her middle was now not so noticeable. She prowled around Jean when she was cooking, bumping against her legs, purring insistently. Jean threw her down little scraps of chicken, slivers of cheese, squeezed the liquid from the tins of tuna she opened to make Ken his sandwiches and poured it straight into her bowl. Mimi followed Jean around the house, but was appalled by the vacuum cleaner. She sat on the window-sill and hissed at it. Later, when Jean sat down to read a magazine, Mimi crept onto her lap, pawed her, tiny claws snagging in the fabric of her cardigan, then settled, sometimes burrowing into the crook of her arm. Or she'd creep up her and rest her head on her chest, her cat's eyes penetrating Jean's.

So Jean was shocked and not a little disappointed when she discovered a little acrid-smelling puddle in the corner of the living room.

'Mimi!' she announced. 'I thought you were properly house-trained!'

The cat came over to investigate. Jean realised there was no point in punishing the little mite. It knew no better. She scrubbed at the carpet with disinfectant, hoping the smell would put the cat off going there again.

Once Mimi had had her injections, Jean knew it was safe to let her out, and watched, fascinated, as the cat stepped gingerly out into the garden, sniffing the air, ears twitching, a breeze ruffling her fur. The garden was rich virgin territory, a fiesta of sights and sounds and smells. Everything was fascinating to her. When a bird landed at the end of the garden Mimi was transfixed. She crouched low, her little body ramrod straight. She wiggled her bottom, preparing. The bird flew away. Jean was disappointed.

Inside, if Jean spread the newspaper out over the table, Mimi would come and sit in the middle, defying Jean to push her off. She never did. If the cat saw any small object on the table – a coin, or a pen, she would jab at it with her paw, once, twice, then with more force, until the object hit the floor with a tiny thud. Jean got into the habit of placing little things by the edge of the table on purpose.

'Mum! Where's my ring? The one I bought from

Warren James? I can't find it anywhere and I'm going to be late!' Chrissie called.

'Umm – do you think it could have rolled under something?'

Hastily Jean got down on her knees and looked under the fridge. There were two plastic balls, the stub of a pencil, several cat biscuits and Chrissie's ring.

'Found it!'

Mimi had enjoyed making it skitter around the linoleum.

Roger and Kay told her Mother wasn't coming round again until she'd got rid of the cat. It wasn't fair – at her age! To be exiled from her daughter's house. And as she knew very well, Roger lived two hundred miles away, and Kay's job kept her so busy, and Jean was her mother's only support.

'I know. I'm sorry,' Jean told them.

'Jean!' Ken shouted. 'That cat's ruining your father's chair! Make it stop.'

Jean ran into the living room where Mimi was sharpening her claws on the base of the chair. It was a good, rough surface, perfect for getting rid of the dead outer scales of claws – better than the scratching post, Jean thought.

'Mimi!' Jean said. 'Stop it.'

The cat carried on.

'Jean!' shouted Ken a few days later. 'You'll never guess what that cat has done!' He was in his study. Jean ran upstairs. Ken was pointing under his desk. There were three tiny turds nestling, gleaming, together.

'Disgusting,' he said. 'You'd better clean it up, Jean. I'm not so sure about that cat. Maybe Roger and Kay have a point.'

Luckily no one was around when Mimi brought in her first mouse. It wasn't dead. At first Jean thought she'd brought it in to play with and look after, like a substitute kitten. That was until Mimi pounced and got it by the neck.

'Out! Out!' Jean opened the back door and shooed Mimi out.

Later she found a headless, dismembered corpse on the back door-step. Jean used a brush and shovel to get rid of it. She discovered she wasn't as squeamish as she thought.

Mimi would sit on the window-sill, observing people in the street, like some woman of the night drumming up custom. She'd watch the neighbours and the cars. Jean joined her. If Mimi saw another cat she'd freeze with attention, watch its every movement. If she saw a bird resting on a tree, Mimi bared her teeth and made a strange chattering noise.

As she grew, the cat was only a very little less active. She liked to go out in the early evening, returning when it was properly dark. Jean missed her when she wasn't there. There was nothing on her lap. She would pluck at the cover of the settee with her fingers, her nails catching the material.

'Stop that,' Ken said. 'You're irritating me.'

One night Mimi didn't come home at all. Jean didn't go to bed until one am. Every ten minutes she stood calling Mimi at the back door.

'Mum!' Everyone will think you're losing it!' Chrissie said. 'You're so embarrassing!'

Eventually Jean had to go to bed not knowing if Mimi was waiting at the back door. They would have to get a cat flap. In the morning, Mimi still hadn't arrived home. Beside herself, Jean combed the neighbouring streets, looking for a black-and-white heap on the road. Nothing.

That evening, fighting back the tears, Jean heard a strange, distorted wail coming from the garden. She ran to the back door, opened it, and there was Mimi, dishevelled, yowling, rolling on the ground. At first Jean thought she'd been injured, but Mimi strutted in, yowled some more, crouched down and presented her backside to the world.

'She's on heat!' Jean realised. 'And only five months old!'

That night Jean was kept awake by the howls of the neighbouring toms. Ken told her the whole thing was getting out of hand, and the cat would have to go. There was to be no argument. His word was final.

The next morning, when Jean was emptying the litter tray, she used the scoop to lift several turds and carefully carried them upstairs to the study, where she placed them under Ken's desk. She stood there for a few moments hardly conscious of her surroundings, her heart palpitating, a steady trickle of adrenalin making her veins come alive. There was a biro on the edge of the desk, and with her index finger, she pushed it and made it roll towards the edge, until it fell.

That afternoon when she got back from work, she was sleepy. There was dinner to put on, but first she thought she would have a nap. A nap in the middle of the day! She heard her mother's disapproving voice, and it was like a relish to her. She curled up on her bed and fell asleep. Mimi came to join her. Later they both sat by the window, watching the world go by.

Jean was hungry. She opened the fridge door and immediately Mimi miaowed. Jean spotted the trifle she'd made last night – Chrissie had gone out but was looking forward to having her share that evening. Jean brought it out, fetched a spoon from the cutlery drawer and tucked in. Mimi looked interested. Jean ran her finger along the cream topping and let Mimi lick it.

It was then she noticed Mimi's nipples. They were pink and protruding. Jean had never even noticed she had nipples up till now. She recalled what had happened to her own breasts when she was pregnant with the kids. They'd swollen like melons, and her nipples had darkened and grown. She tingled with the memory; was Mimi pregnant?

If so, Mimi wasn't telling. Jean bought a book about cats and kittens from the Oxfam shop and read it from cover to cover. She was appalled and fascinated to learn that female cats on heat have many different partners – the new kittens could have several different fathers. In one night Mimi had had more lovers than she had ever had. Because she'd been asking for it.

Mimi wasn't telling, and nor was Jean. Since Mimi only ever sat on her lap – Ken shooed her off, Chrissie was worried she'd leave cat hair on her clothes – only Jean could feel the little squirms and ripples that indicated the presence of foetal kittens. Neither Ken nor Chrissie took account of Mimi's increased girth. They just assumed Jean was over feeding her.

Jean was worried about what would happen when Mimi's time came. Already the cat was getting less active. She didn't always want to go out in the evening. Jean was upset to see the change in her. She loved it when Mimi shot around the room as if she was on fire. Jean knew from her own experience, once the kittens were born, Mimi's life would be over. She'd just be a kitten-feeding machine. It wasn't fair.

Mimi's black furry toy mouse was lying by Jean's feet on the carpet. She pushed it with her toe. She pounced on it, picked it up and placed it on the armchair. She realised there were preparations to be made.

Cats like to give birth in seclusion, she'd read.

She found an old suitcase in the garage that should have been thrown out. She took it up to her bedroom. Cats need bedding when they're nursing – something soft and comforting, something that maybe smelt of their owner. Jean found an old black dress of hers that she'd never wear again – it was far too revealing and Ken, Damon and Chrissie had complained when she'd worn it just the once. She put that in the suitcase, together with a négligé and some old underwear. Then she hid it.

Cats are pregnant for nine weeks, or sixty-three days. Jean knew pretty much exactly when the kittens would be born. In the previous week she went out to the supermarket and bought special food for nursing queens. She was in no hurry to go home. She liked to go out to the supermarket just when it was getting dark, and stay there until it was night. It was calming to wander the aisles. She liked the cosmetics section. She examined a certain red lipstick, and bristled when another woman came over and picked up the same shade. She felt as if her territory had been invaded.

What Jean most admired about Mimi was her independence. Although Jean was making the necessary preparations, the fact was, Mimi would be perfectly capable of looking after herself, or doing the whole thing alone. Cats were all instinct – and they did only whatever it was they wanted to do. Not what anybody else wanted them to do. Jean knew that, as much as Mimi valued her company and cooking skills, she wasn't vital to her. She could survive without her. Cats, basically, didn't give a fuck.

!!!

Jean had used a swear word inside her head. Fuck. It sounded quite good. She didn't give a fuck. That wasn't a word that she and Ken ever used. They talked about 'going to bed early'. But other people had fucks. Cats did.

Mimi was really heavy now. She spent as much time as she could on the settee. Jean didn't bother to remove the matted collection of black-and-white hair.

'Honestly, Mum,' Chrissie said. 'Ever since you've got that cat and Grandma's stopped coming, you've let yourself go!'

It was Saturday night. Ken was watching the satellite channel with that antiques programme. Chrissie was out. Jean realised Mimi wasn't around. Puzzled, she looked in the kitchen, the dining room, then upstairs. Mimi was on their bed. She mewed a greeting to Jean and got awkwardly up. Jean went to stroke her. Below her was an unmistakable damp patch.

Her waters have broken, Jean realised.

The time had come. She hurried to the wardrobe and got out the suitcase. She'd put some of the make-up she'd bought from Tesco's in there too. The lipstick was perhaps a shade too red. Well, I don't give a fuck, Jean thought. Not a flying fuck.

She wriggled into the black dress. It still fitted her. And, yes, the neckline plunged far too low. Mimi stared at Jean, her eyes beady and alarmed.

'You'll be fine,' Jean told the cat.

Suddenly a wave of heat coursed through her. Was it a hot flush? Because she was that age. No – this heat felt different. It was hormonal, no doubt about that, but a different kind of hormonal.

She took the suitcase and went quietly down the stairs. She was so warm, she didn't need a coat. The latch on the front door snicked behind her. In front of her, a short drive away, were the bright lights of the city, its clubs, its back alleys – those toms.

Jean tingled with anticipation, with liquid excitement. She might have left it a bit late for this sort of thing, but what was time, really? Mimi started early, and she would start late. Money wasn't a problem. She'd helped herself to a portion of their building-society savings only that morning. She could ring in sick at work.

She thought of the men out there – all waiting for her. Her teeth chattered with delight. She was as taut as a bow, but wriggled her bottom sinuously.

Mimi shuddered as the first kitten squeezed its way out of her onto Jean's bed. She licked its bloody body and saw to the placenta.

Jean walked into the basement club and checked in her suitcase, adjusted her hair, and already she'd caught the attention of a well-turned-out man by the bar.

Then came the second. The first was already sucking greedily. A third. A fourth. Finally a fifth. Mimi purred loudly.

Ken discovered her. 'Jean! JEAN! The bloody cat's gone and had kittens – on our bed! Jean! JEAN!'

'So tell me. What's your name, honey?' the man crooned, as he gazed down into Jean's cleavage.

'Mimi,' she purred.

# MICHELLE GREEN
## Forklift Trucks: a Brief Guide

'Okay. It's your turn, Lydia. When the call comes through I'll hold it while you pick a, b, c or d, as we agreed. Write your choice on a stick-it and pass it over to me, and then I'll transfer the call to you. You get it right, we keep going round. You get it wrong, you have to go out and get the doughnuts.'

It's call-centre roulette with Donna as referee. She pushes a button on her phone and nods to me. I pass over my piece of paper and my headset beeps as the call comes through.

'Good morning GF Shnier Western Canada Customer Services Lydia speaking how may I help you?' I breathe in and wait for the voice. Will it be:

The hard-sell, customer-licking sales manager,

The squeaky new guy,

The wrong number, OR

The scaly salesman with the voice that turns a linoleum order into contemplation of harassment charges?

He starts to speak and I roll my eyes up to the ceiling. Shit. That's the third time this week I've been stuck with the doughnut run because of the goddam temp at Open Floors Ltd. Fucking redial- speakerphone thing. Why do they keep hiring people who find using the telephone such a massive challenge? Donna is laughing through her closed mouth as I feel my sense of humour slipping away. I DON'T GET PAID ENOUGH FOR THIS.

'Have a nice day, sir.' Have a nice nice, sir. Nice a nice nice. Nice? Ahh yes – so very – nice – and – definitive of my life. Please. Have another doughnut.

Call again soon. Bubye now. Thank you. *Ciao*. *Hasta manãna*. *Au revoir*. Till we next speak. Later. See ya. (Wouldn't wanna be ya.) How many ways can you tell someone to fuck off without using those two words? It's all in the smile you paste on over the phone: all teeth, no eyes. I don't believe it – he's still on the line. No really, it's fine. WHY ARE WE STILL TALKING? No not at all. That's what we're here for. Please feel free to call again if you require any HELP! or account information. We're happy to HELP ME! Whatever you need. WHAT – WHAT AM I DOING HERE?

I spin my chair around and drop in on the bonding session that Sherry's holding across the top of her miniwall. She has mastered the art of cyclical breathing, which enables her to chatter for hours with only the slightest of pauses. It is quite an incredible skill and could probably be put to good use in some other situation – perhaps in the intensive-care ward when the emotionally spent relatives of comatose patients need to slip out to get some rest. Here, however, her verbal talent is more of a liability. The rest of us have learnt to spot the rare moments when she does have to take in more oxygen, and use those little cat flaps of opportunity to either make an escape or launch into our own monologues.

Today she's full of the joys of spring, with a new set of ears that have not yet experienced her unique brand of workplace conversation. The big-haired New Girl is sitting rigidly in her chair with a painful look of interest pasted on her face. So far Sherry's managed to cover all of her major childhood traumas, failed relationships and a small selection of personal theories on life and the universe.

New Girl has just been transferred from head office, allegedly against her will, and is still feigning

104

interest as Sherry introduces her next topic.

'My inner child has a scab on one knee and a yellow T-shirt with *Waikiki '84 Surf's Up* written on the front in a pre-Windows block font.' Sherry's into self-discovery. She's never been to Hawaii. Her neighbours passed the shirt over the fence after they came back from their winter vacation. Last week she was so stressed out by her inner child, I asked her if she needed anyone to baby-sit for the evening. She said she'd think about it.

'I've decided to take surfing lessons to see if I can make contact with her through constructive play. Of course it's not easy to find someone to teach me here, what with being six-hundred and seventy-three kilometres from the West Coast, but y'know, I think even with dry-land surfing I may be able to access a lot of blocked childhood ambition. Anyway, I can't go to Vancouver. Too humid. Bad for my skin.'

I break into a loud slow-motion yawn and stare at the pearl studs hanging unevenly from Sherry's ear-lobes. New Girl glances over with a desperate plea in her eyes and I turn back to my desk. Not my problem, sweetheart. You'll figure it out soon enough. Avoid eye contact, and don't be afraid to be as blunt as a mallet. On days that drag as much as this one I find that practising passive-aggressive bitchiness with my co-workers is even more stimulating than triple-brewed economy coffee. It does get old fast though, and then you have to reheat it in the microwave.

'Good morning GF Shnier Western Canada Customer Services Lydia speaking how may I HELP you?' I lift my eyes up off the screen and make brief contact with Maryann – one pane of glass and several pay scales away from my mid-office pen island/desk. She's scanning the room with management-degree drop-out eyes.

'So that's 72 by 51 of 55293 at $13.17 per square metre.' She lifts her Solitaire™-cramped hand from her mouse and proceeds to pick at a clump of mascara on her lower left lash line. La la la la.

'That'll be shipped by Torpedo via Toronto, and you can expect it by next Wednesday.' The funny thing about her goldfish-window office is that the more authority the little fishy tries to effect, the more she looks on the verge of floating belly-first up to the fluorescent-lighting panel.

'I'm afraid the truck is just not physically capable of crossing three time zones in twelve hours, sir. It's a simple matter of physics, and as much as I would LOVE to . . .' Through the smudged glass Maryann looks like a maiden of the sea – washed up on the shoreline, dead and bloated. She's been surviving on doughnut crumbs for weeks now, which, in combination with the flattering and comfortable lighting, just adds to her Frankenstein-aquarium mystique.

'Certainly, sir. I'll put you through to my manager immediately. I'd like to take this opportunity to thank you for calling GF Shnier Western Canada Customer Services. Haveanicedayholdplease.'

The hold music is a constant source of amusement to me. It's tuned into the radio and so at the mercy of whoever gets into the office first and activates the phone system. I've been working early shifts all month and so I leave my dissatisfied customer to sing the 'my-woman's-gone-left-me-for-my-only-dog' blues for a moment so I can sync up with Maryann. It's time for her scheduled coffee break and I'm ready for her as always. Both hands on the desk, up comes her bloated mer-princess frame from the chair, foot around the side and – TRANSFER. Smooth as Torvill and Dean I pass him on and she picks him up, twisting her body and her face back to the ringing phone. Beautiful, Maryann. Just beautiful. I've cleared my flashing lights. The Russian judges look happy. It's time for a break.

As I pull my earpiece cord-first from my head I see Sales Slug of the Month looming in the doorway. Jon without an 'h' is a master of the dubious art of unwanted innuendo, and here I am – no call on my phone, no burlap cubicle walls for protection – a sitting duck ready for a bad line. In the second it takes for my fight-or-flight impulse to kick in he's on to me. Jon's eyes slither across the room and he moves in my direction with an invertebrate ease. A polycotton-clad buttock slides onto my desk in what he assumes to be a sexy intro and he leans in. He has a <wink> very important customer who should be calling soon. I promise to take care of it <wink> and he saunters off like he's one more smirk away from a blowjob behind the stationery cupboard.

Being dedicated first and foremost to outstanding customer service for imaginary fellatio kings, I pass the main phone box on the way to the can and make a small adjustment for clarity. Nothing an <wink> important client needs more than ten minutes of hold music that's just slightly off the station and in a country kinda vein. Yee haw.

Two steps later I'm through the office doors and into the main warehouse. Hundreds of rolls of carpet lie on huge metal shelves that reach up to the ceiling three storeys above my head, their ends lined up like pieces of giant sidewalk chalk. I walk past the main loading dock and over to the back corner where John with an 'h' is shrink-wrapping a pile of vinyl floor tiles to a wooden pallet. He speeds up the machine when he sees me and shouts through the gaps in his teeth.

'Sent Little Dave out to Vancouver on one of

these.' He smiles the sprawling smile of a man with very little to lose and continues yelling over the noise.

'Shrink-wrapped him to a pallet and threw him on the overnight truck. Boy was he mad!' John stops the machine, throws his head back and laughs right up into the deep recesses of the ceiling. He's worked in this warehouse for close to fifteen years and has the missing digits to prove it.

'What you doin' back here, Lyd? The dragon lady let you out of your pen to check up on the lowlife?'

'Yeah. I'm here on a safety spot check. One more summer student gets locked in the back of the trailer and it's your ass, mister. Those are her words, of course, not mine.' I keep my face still and wait expectantly for his 'I'm dealing with management' voice. He doesn't disappoint.

'Well you tell her that I'm incredibly flattered but have to respectfully decline the request for my ass. Don't think the wife would be too happy about that. Hey listen – you still want that forklift lesson?'

John knows about the serial boredom involved in an office job and has decided to covertly redeploy me into the warehouse since I've shown an interest in driving the machines. My motivations are not entirely pure, as they mostly revolve around a recurring fantasy I have about driving the forks straight through the wall of Maryann's fishbowl and pinning her to the window until she bursts a gill. When I told John about that he launched into a lecture about how a forklift is a potentially dangerous machine that should not be used in anger. He thought I should go for something more subtle, like rat poison. I argued that she was probably immune but he seemed to think that chemical intervention would be the better path to take. Anyway – I was to commence driving lessons twice a week during the management and sales meetings. We both figured that they'd all be too distracted with trying to out-jargon each other to notice a renegade office worker tooling around the warehouse on a one-tonne truck. It turns out we were right. Last Thursday was the start of my new life as a forklift-capable woman and although I hadn't totally wrapped my head around the backwards steering I was picking it up remarkably well, or so I was told.

'How about another lesson this afternoon then? There's a meeting at two, and Donna said she'd cover for me.'

'Yep. Sounds good.'

The shrink-wrapper revs up again as I turn and head back to my desk.

I spend another half hour talking to irate salesmen and picking the dirt from under my nails. Donna has sent Sherry out for doughnuts as apparently she cannot function without a little jam-filled happiness, and so the office noise has dulled to a series of clicks, beeps and mechanical phone chat. Just as I feel tears of boredom welling up beneath my eyes the red numbers on my phone flicker and change to 2:00pm, and I bounce from my seat faster than a bad cheque. At long last. Maryann's safely out of reach in the meeting room, locked away for a few hours with a flipchart and a room full of people each with an axe to grind and the corresponding PowerPoint presentation with which to do it. I skip into the warehouse with visions of industrial drag races in my head. It's gonna be a great afternoon – free from socially inept customers and performance-target anxiety – and my mouth curls up into a smile as I head for the loading bay.

Three of the four docks have half-filled trailers backed up to the edge and the fourth gapes wide and empty, spilling sunlight and dust into the huge dark space I'm in. I'm amazed again at the power of natural light; even the industrial wasteland across the road has a real beauty to it at this time of the day. The colours fade slightly like the seams in John's old jeans and the heat moves in waves across the tarmac. A Big Mac container untangles itself from the chain link fence at the edge of the parking lot and two steps across the little window I've got to the outside world.

'Hell – ooo! Ready to burn some rubber?' My partner in crime is smiling big and toothless as he pulls up and parks the red Raymond truck with a flourish.

'Okay. So you remember all the basics we went over last week. Just go easy on the power until you get the hang of the steering again. You've got thirty-foot clearance on all sides; there won't be any more loading traffic for at least an hour, so the bay is yours. I'm gonna grab a coffee. Be right back.' A proud-parent look crosses his face as he turns and whistles his way over to the kitchen.

I step up to the controls. It feels heavy under my hands until I press lightly on the foot pedal. The motor kicks in and I move backwards in a graceful arc – one hundred and eighty degrees in three seconds. My hands are still confused by the steering column and I spend a minute covering the same six feet of space, backwards, then forwards. I remember what John told me about suspending my logic and just feeling the way it wants to move. Turn right to go left, turn left to go right. Right to left, left to right. It's not long until I'm in a meditative state with this large piece of metal, circling back on myself and letting the straight lines of the office fade with the blinding light from the open dock behind me. Right to left, left to right.

'There you go!' John bellows praise from across the warehouse and I look up grinning. I pull the truck around to show him my impeccable right turn and as the storage shelves pass before me I catch sight of his opposite number, Jon without an 'h', swaggering across to the meeting room, files in hand. He swivels his head in my direction and I cringe as he flashes his custom leer at my chest, winking and pursing his lips on his way past. Slimy asshole. I rev the engine in time with my telepathic glare: move that spotty ass out of my sight, little man. He picks up my message and twitches like a cockroach when the lights come on mid-feed, scuttling away and round the corner. I grit my teeth and vow to get myself out of this dump before the year is up. At this point, toothless John is the only person standing between me and my execution of a workplace massacre. I pull the candy-red machine back to face him.

'Acid off a duck's back, Lyd. Heh he he – acid off a duck's back. Nice turn by the way.' John swigs from his cup and stares in the direction the Roachman made his exit. I'm about to crack a joke to confirm that we've moved on when John freezes for half a second – cup at a forty-five degree angle to his mouth, bottom lip hanging down slightly. The sharp click of heels echoes across the concrete floor. I can hear voices, low and urgent, and the heels speed up. It's Maryann and the Roach. They round the corner like their collective tight ass is on fire and march in our direction with military precision. Maryann's got me on her radar and she's moving so quickly that her bouffant hairdo is barely able to keep up the pace.

'Lydia! John!'

We both breathe in slowly before John jumps in with a winning smile and the defence.

'Maryann. So glad you could make it. We have decided to proactively enhance the breadth of our employee skill base and begin cross-task training with a view to broadening the qualification pool in the workplace . . . and so, um . . . I was hoping we could meet with you before the day was out to give you a preview of the progress that Lyd – Lydia is making on the trucks. What luck! It seems you have been able to take time out from your management duties to –'

Maryann's eyes cut through John and straight to me. She's blazing with anger and I'm replaying the conversation I had with her a month ago about forklift training. The details are somewhat hazy, but the words 'inappropriate use of time' and 'without question, NO' do spring to mind. Oh yeah, and the 'difficulty accepting supervisory direction' note that was quoted from my last performance review.

'Lydia. I would like you to explain to me what exactly you are doing at this precise moment.' She opens her eyes wide and I notice for the first time that they are the exact colour of dried seaweed. Roach hovers behind her with one thumb hooked across his belt, his index finger casually pointing down the crease of his pants to his crotch.

'Well, Maryann, at this precise moment I am in the process of learning to drive a forklift truck.' Maryann's face is turning beet red, showing up a network of spider veins through the thick layer of beige powder. Her lips part slightly in an involuntary twitch that shows her tiny pointed teeth. I wonder, does she file them, or are they naturally cannibalistic in shape? I take another breath and keep going.

'Actually that's not entirely true. At THIS precise moment I am engaged in employer/employee feedback, which of course I welcome as an important tool for my personal and professional growth.'

John coughs beside me and I get another flash of Maryann's carnivorous teeth. Her mouth starts to move in tight little gestures like a contracting anus and I turn down the volume. Here it comes. Let me guess . . . verbal warning, maybe even a written warning this time. Excellent, it'd be great to get some more paper in my file. More paper. More and more and more of it. That's what makes an office run efficiently really, doesn't it. That and a slow and steady stream of sexual harassment from a seemingly endless parade of men in cheap suits. What more could an employee ask for? Benefits? A decent wage? Promotional prospects? Positive feedback? Appreciation from management? A boss who contributes more to the office than a slight increase in carbon dioxide levels? Really. WHAT MORE COULD I ASK FOR??? A FUCKING LIFE PERHAPS?

The metal of the steering lever feels cold in my hand and as the rest of me heats up I choke on my own breath. Muscles contract.

WHAT – WHAT AM I DOING HERE?

The question rings loud in my ears as I press my foot to the ground and pull hard to the left. The motor kicks in and I feel myself being pulled round fast, past my boss, past my potential rapist, past the depressing backdrop to my Monday to Friday, past my concerns about money and security, past the abandoned goals left lying at the front door, past the only goddam friend I ever had in this place, and towards an opening. I'm gunning the motor, heading for this gift of an exit. The static voices in the warehouse get louder, then shriller, and my escape gets bigger and brighter before me. As the forks clear the edge of the dock I release my foot from the pedal and grip the frame tight with both hands. The waves of heat hit my skin and wash all the colours out of me. I am indulged with exactly three seconds of airborne doubt before gravity turns me and the truck into thirteen broken bones, a redundancy package and a liability claim that would leave the thick treads of my tyres smeared permanently up Maryann's back.

On behalf of no one but myself, this is Lydia speaking. Good afternoon, thank you for calling, and have a nice day.

# CHRIS SCHOLES
## Mouse Ears

Six months ago, Laura agreed to marry Pearson. I wish she hadn't but there it is. I have heard from a friend, that she heard from a friend, that it is rumoured that Pearson has a piercing in an intimate part of his body. From the very first time I heard it I think of Pearson as Pearson the Penis Piercer. This is not good; he is going to become my brother-in-law in a few weeks. Panic sets in as Pearson the Penis Piercer burns itself into my brain; it is becoming a reflex arc. Every time someone mentions his name, I fill in the gaps.

As soon as my sister announced that she was going to get married, my mother took to looking through all the old photographs. Out of a cardboard box came our first steps, our first day at school and birthday cakes with increasing numbers of candles. It seemed to me that she needed to remind herself of her history; she wanted to look at what she'd achieved before she sat back and waited for the next generation to arrive. My mother still believed that our family was the kind you read about in story-books. We were all destined to live happily ever after in a cotton-wool world of happy families, frilly frocks and smiling children.

She stacked little piles of snaps in an order only she could understand around the kitchen. Her wedding photographs, with my father looking stiff and edgy, were on a chair, my grandparents lived next to a value bag of carrots and the ones on the table were swept away like fallen leaves from our family tree whenever she needed the space to put down a hot plate.

'Here's one of you trying to make a Womble, Shaz.' I had called in to see her on my way home from work. 'And here's another of you wearing that flamenco dress you made out of an old lace table-cloth tucked into your knickers.' She gave me one of her proud looks. 'I knew then you'd grow up to be a designer.'

She didn't know of course, but it did make all this photograph sifting a bit clearer; she was reliving our childhood and the life she'd once led. Slotting together the pieces that had led to one of her daughters getting married, although I suspect that she was wishing that it were I who had found a husband.

I sat munching my way through a plate full of chocolate digestives unaware of what was to come next.

'Laura wants to ask you something.'

'Well she knows where I live,' I replied. All this talk about Laura's wedding was starting to get on my nerves.

'But she's afraid you might say no.'

'What's she so scared of?' I was on my guard now.

'She wants you to make her wedding dress for her.'

'Oh, no,' I said, smiling and shaking my head at the same time, 'that's one thing I won't do. No wonder she was afraid to ask.'

The following weekend the three of us were out shopping. Laura in her element, holding lace against satin for her dress and white muslin against floral prints for mine, an unwilling bridesmaid. I still hadn't agreed to make her wedding dress but it didn't seem to matter any more. No one had the faintest intention of taking no for an answer and besides, the smell that drifted up from the rolls of fabric had drugged me into a quiet submission.

It takes all day for Laura to choose what material I am to sew up into the dress she has been dreaming about since she was fourteen. She tests fabrics for their floatiness, their translucency. She doesn't consider it necessary to ask me if I will have any problems stitching it. Just as my mother is about to sign the cheque, Laura turns to me and asks if I would be able to incorporate a few mouse ears into the design.

'Oh!' exclaims my mother. 'Mouse ears would be lovely.'

A few more yards of pearl satin are rolled out, the scissors once more making their satisfying crunch, and I am pulled into their trap a little bit further.

My mother had found a photograph of me making mouse ears. They were really supposed to be rose petals but Laura thought that they looked like mouse ears and the name stuck. Laura thinks that hundreds of hand-stitched petals scattered delicately and anchored where they fall on her train will be quite magical. It is going to take a miracle for me to finish the dress in time.

Suddenly our parcels of shopping have become so precious, they require a taxi to carry them home. My mother forks out for that as well. When we get back, we walk straight into the lounge, fall into armchairs and kick off our shoes. Laura closes her eyes and says, 'Thank goodness that's all over and done with.' Who is she kidding?

I soon discover that the problem with making a wedding dress is that it takes over the whole house. My flat is filled with white froth and three hundred and fifty mouse ears. Everything has to be kept perfectly clean, cooking smells are absolutely banned and Laura doesn't want the dress to smell of my perfume on her big day.

She calls at the flat to be measured. 'Pearson can't stand fat brides,' she sighs.

Would that be Pearson the Penis Piercer she's talking about?

'So I'm going to go on a diet.'

This is dangerous talk for a seamstress. If she goes on a diet, I will have to allow for a possible loss of weight.

'I think I should be able to lose about a stone in a month if I work at it.'

The thought crosses my mind that if she looks thinner, then I'm going to look fatter. It is entirely possible that she is doing this not to please Pearson but to spite me. I resign myself to the fact that I'm going to have to go on a diet too.

I add an inch or two to her measurements as I call them out and Laura decides to walk the three miles home to burn off a few calories.

I am going to eat nothing but cottage cheese and salad for the next month.

A few days later, my mother phones for a progress report. She has had another lovely idea. I groan but she is obviously going to ignore any protest I might make. She wants to know if it would be possible to incorporate a couple of box pleats into the front of the skirt. I can't imagine why anyone would be asking for such a thing, but she tells me that she had them in the front of her wedding dress and her mother did too. It would mean such a lot to her. This dress is going to have as many memories stitched into it as there are in her beloved photographs.

'What does Laura say?' My mother ignores the real meaning of my question and tells me that Laura says that she's lost four pounds. She's bought a skipping rope because aerobic exercise is the best for fat burning.

'By the way.'

'Yes Mum?'

'I've bought a new bathroom mat and it just matches my wedding shoes. Isn't that strange?'

I can't think of an answer.

'Just thought you'd like to know,' she chirps, and then hangs up on me.

The second week Laura lost five pounds and the third week she managed to shed four more. Despite a mountain of salad every day I had only managed two in total. I took the dress in and cursed every stitch. On the night I attached the mouse ears to the train, it was four in the morning before I managed to crawl into bed.

Seven days to go and the dress was ready. I needed Laura to call round and try it on for the last time before the wedding. My mother decided that this was such an important family event that she would come and bring my dad to take a few photographs. Laura was late; we sat and drank tea fearful that we might splash the dress that was hanging from the door frame wrapped in a white sheet.

'I never noticed before,' my mother said looking around her, 'how clean you keep this place. I wouldn't like to think you're coming down with that tidying-up illness.' I assured her that there was no chance of that.

'Still,' she sniffed, 'it's a bit too clean for my liking. You would tell me if you had a problem wouldn't you Shaz?' I assured her that I would.

Laura arrived, glowing from the run in the park she'd taken on her way over.

'I'll just use your shower and then I'll be ready,' she said breaking into a girlish giggle.

I dressed her in my bedroom whilst Mum and

Dad waited for her to make her grand entrance. Even though I say it myself, the dress was a triumph. I opened the door and she floated into the lounge.

'Oh, Laura,' my mother choked, 'you are so beautiful.'

Laura stood proudly in the middle of the room and gave her a twirl.

'If only your father could see you now.'

As my father was standing right next to her at the time, this was a little bit disconcerting.

'Take a photograph quick,' she encouraged, 'I don't want to lose the moment.'

Laura preened and displayed, smiled for the camera and admired her new figure in front of my mirror. Finally she managed to offer me a quick thank you.

'Right,' I said, 'I only have to tidy a couple of stitches up and then we're done.' I heaved the dress over Laura's head, coaxed it back onto its hanger and wrapped it up. Then I went into the kitchen and brought out a plate full of chocolate éclairs.

'Time to celebrate.'

'I couldn't possibly,' said Laura gazing hungrily at the plate. 'But I'd really love one.'

'Everyone knows that brides get so nervous before their wedding that they lose weight without even trying.' This was a welcome comment from my mother. Laura took a cake, and ate it, then the rest of us joined in. It was one of those happy family moments when everything has finally come together. We didn't even need to take a photograph. Two bottles of wine and a helping of cheese and biscuits later, they left for home. Laura looked radiant but my mother outshone her.

I cleaned the house again, swept the floor clear of crumbs, washed my hands and scrubbed my nails.

I went to bed and had the best night's sleep I'd had in weeks. The following morning I phoned work and said that I thought I was coming down with the flu and wouldn't be in for a day or so. Then I took the dress down from the door, laid it carefully on the floor and sliced open the side seams with a razor blade. An hour later, I had cut an inch and a half off each side. It took two full days to stitch it back together. When I'd finished, the dress looked as good on the inside as it did on the outside. It was the most satisfying two days I had ever had. I had forgotten food, forgotten drink and I'd even forgotten the wedding. When my father came to collect the dress, he brought me flowers and a card. Inside it read, 'We will never forget what you have done for your sister. All our love, Mum and Dad.'

Saturday arrived together with cards and bouquets and hairdressers and cakes. I sat with my father and drank coffee and cognacs whilst my mother scurried around upstairs and Laura languished in the bath. An hour before we were all to leave for the church, Laura put on her dress. I had rehearsed my part well.

'Laura, what have you been doing to yourself?'
'Nothing, why?'
'I can't zip your dress up.'
My mother flew into the bedroom.
'I hope you haven't gone and got pregnant just to spoil my day!'

Laura stood in front of the mirror unable to believe what she saw. The dress that had fitted her perfectly only a few days ago, now struggled to keep her flesh from escaping.

'What's Pearson going to say when he sees me in this?' she wailed.

You'll soon find out, I thought.

Pearson watched as his bride walked down the

aisle towards him, a weak smile on his lips.

'You look lovely,' he managed to whisper to Laura.

'Sod off!' her reply.

The congregation sat down and admired the flutter of mouse ears on her train.

'Do you Pearson Anthony Palmer . . .'

Pearson Anthony Penis Piercer Palmer?

'Do you Laura Elizabeth . . .'

Sod off

'Metcalfe . . .'

They did. Laura turned around to hand me her flowers and the dress groaned under the strain. She saw the happiness in my eyes.

'You bitch,' she muttered a little too loudly, attracting the vicar's attention to a possible hitch in the ceremony. 'I'll never forgive you for this.'

'I know,' I whispered.

# CATH STAINCLIFFE
## Riviera

I never think of myself as a murderer. And it was never my idea. It was Geoffrey's from the get-go. She was his mother. It would never have happened if it had just been me. Does that sound feeble? I suppose I was – feeble – for long enough. But killing someone – well, that wasn't feeble.

At first it was just comments. Mutterings and murmurings about how Nora was an albatross round our necks and how she would live to get a telegram from the Queen just to spite him. I let it wash over me. Kept my own counsel. After the redundancy – that's when it changed. He began working out all these elaborate plans. I thought he was joking for long enough but then it wasn't funny any more. Deadly serious.

Geoffrey's always been one for those forensic programmes on the telly. Normally he's a bit squeamish; he'd never watch an operation, say, and if he cuts himself shaving or even gets a spell in his finger from the garden he's all theatrical sighs and wincing and pale sweaty brow. He can't watch me quarter a chicken or clean a fish. But as long as there's a forensic side to it, something to do with crime and punishment, then he's as happy as Larry; up to his eyeballs in blood and gore.

He turned to me one night after *CSI*, where they'd nailed this fella because he'd left dandruff at the murder scene, and he said, 'She'd have to disappear.'

I stopped knitting (I was doing a lovely matinée jacket for the girl next-door who was due soon) and I stared at him.

'We'd have to get rid of the body. . . but we'd plan it first so that people expected her to go.'

I frowned. 'Like she was ill or something you mean?'

'No!' He sighed and put on his patience-of-a-saint expression. 'If she got ill and died we'd have to have a doctor and a post-mortem. The science these days . . .' He broke off with a snort and waved in the direction of the telly. 'People can *think* she's died but actually we'll have . . . disposed of her.' He wasn't smiling. I was waiting for a punch line – but it never came. 'So,' he pushed his recliner further upright and leant towards me, 'we start off telling people Nora's moved, gone to Filey. . .'

'She hates Filey.'

'Scarborough then, Whitby, wherever. Just concentrate, Pamela.'

He hates being interrupted.

'Then a bit later we say she's had a heart attack and died and she wanted her ashes scattering at sea.'

I laughed at that. It didn't sound like Nora. She was nervous of water. I remembered when Geoffrey and I were courting and he was still living at Nora's the three of us had shared a holiday together. Torbay, the English Riviera. It was wonderful, the sun cracking the flags and the houses with palm trees and restaurants with lights outside and warm enough to eat alfresco. We even saw Max Bygraves, he had a big place up on the hills and we saw him in his Rolls; I think it was a Rolls but I've never been very good with cars.

Anyway Nora would spend all day on the beach building up to a dip, said she was waiting for the sun to warm the sea up. Then when the beach was emptying and the water was still, she'd wade in until the water was up to her waist and stand there. Never went deeper, never got her shoulders wet.

Her brother had drowned when they were children. She told me that week in Devon, after dinner one night. Only time I heard her mention him. They lived up in Harpurhey, big family, nine of them in all. Harold, that was her little brother, he followed the bigger ones to the canal one day. They weren't allowed to go in, it was full of muck and rubbish and God-knows-what from the mills, but the lads would dare each other and the big 'uns would jump in until someone saw and chased them away.

Harold was larking about with a bit of old chain at the side and he just tripped. He sank like a stone. Only five. Those that could swim tried to find him while Nora watched from the bank. But he'd gone and they had to fetch his parents from the mill.

Nora had clamped her mouth tight then, when she was telling me, and wiped her eyes and smoothed the table-cloth and then started stacking the cups and saucers like she was at home. We used to talk a bit before Geoffrey and I got married, then it all changed.

'She can't swim,' I pointed out, 'she wouldn't want her ashes in the sea.'

'There wouldn't be any ashes, would there,' Geoffrey snapped.

I didn't want to listen to any more of his stupid fantasies so put my knitting away and stood up.

'We'd have to do it somewhere neutral, somewhere they'd never connect to us,' Geoffrey said, following me into the kitchen. 'Then dispose of . . . the evidence.'

'How?'

He looked a little uncomfortable. 'There are ways: quarries, dumps . . . easier if it's in smaller sections.'

I'd an image of Geoffrey with my rubber gloves

and a freezer knife. I shook my head. 'And then what?'

'We'd be able to sort all this out,' he waved his hand round the kitchen. 'Settle her estate . . .'

Estate? A two-up-two-down in Ladybarn and a life-insurance policy. I told Geoffrey. 'Not without a death certificate, we wouldn't.'

And he thinks he's the clever one.

I really thought he'd seen sense after that. But then a few weeks later when there was nothing on telly, he switched it off and came and sat next to me on the sofa. That was very odd. Well, both things were odd: the telly never went off, not before bed, and the sofa was my space really, he had his recliner. For a moment I thought he was going to tell me he'd met someone else or had cancer or something.

'Pamela,' he says, 'I've worked it all out.' And he launches into a big explanation. How we tell people that Nora is going to stay with us for a bit, that her nerves are bad, the house is getting too much for her, and then a few weeks later we tell them she's very low and talking about doing something silly and the doctor's worried. 'Then,' he says, 'we need to find a believable way for it to look like suicide. She's too frail to hang herself. And I don't see how we could get a bottle of Paracetamol down her.'

He was right, she ate like a bird, you could hardly grind it into her food.

'Women usually do it in the bath,' I said, 'easier to clean up.'

He went white then. Combination of blood and nudity, I shouldn't wonder. Got up and stalked out.

I thought if I kept raising obstacles he'd give up.

Next thing we had a run of bills: car insurance, MOT, the water rates went up, the TV licence was due.

Geoffrey spent hours at the dining-room table, sifting through papers, stabbing at a calculator and sighing.

One day after lunch I tackled him. 'We could sell the house.'

'What?'

'We don't need a place this size any more. Somewhere smaller, it'd be more economical, easier to run.'

'This is our asset,' he blustered, like I'd suggested he sell his body.

'Well, maybe now's the time to use it.'

'It doesn't work like that.' Geoffrey always says this when he wants to stop you talking about something.

'It can do. If you'd only just think about it!' I knew I sounded shrill but it upset me. The way he never gave me any credit. I know I'm not well educated and I was never a manager or anything like that but I'm not stupid. Geoffrey thinks everyone who doesn't agree with him one hundred per cent is stupid. I reckon I'd beat him in a proper IQ test, any time. It was like that with Nora, we all knew Nora was a bit slow, she could barely read and sometimes it took her a while to grasp something new but she coped perfectly well. She'd raised Geoffrey on her own after his father died, and looked after him well and held a job as a machinist for over thirty years. She was still capable. But not according to Geoffrey.

'Or Nora could sell up and move in here,' I said.

'What?' He grimaced. 'We'd all go mad!'

'Why?'

'Her wittering on and her bloody Bingo, she'd fill the place with cats and fag ends. She's losing her marbles as it is . . .'

'She could have her own room. We could make it *en suite*.'

'*En suite*!  She doesn't even know the meaning of the word.'  He could be very vitriolic and it wasn't good for him; his face all red and spit in the corners of his mouth.

'So?!  She's not that bad.  I wouldn't mind.  It would sort the future out for all of us.'

'She'd ruin our lives and you know it.  I can't think why you even raised it as a possibility.  It won't be long till she needs constant care.  Be a bloody nightmare.'

'Better than murder,' I muttered and left him to it.

I wouldn't care but it wasn't as if our position was desperate.  Okay, there was no salary since his redundancy but if we budgeted really carefully we could manage on the interest from the savings plans he'd set up.  The mortgage was paid off so it was only bills really.  Granted there'd be no holidays and we'd have to keep an eye on the heating, perhaps trade the car in but it was hardly as if we were going to be made homeless or go hungry.

I had one more go at him.  Phyllis had told me about a scheme that she and Terry had signed up to when he had to go private for his op.  In effect they'd sold their house to a building society but they could live in it for the rest of their lives.  There was even provision for home nursing and the like.  'It's not as if we've anyone to pass it on to,' Phyllis said.

Same as me and Geoffrey: we never had children, just never happened.  Phyllis and Terry had a boy, Jack, but he died as a toddler.  Flu, would you believe.  I think of that every time we have our jabs.

So, I tried telling Geoffrey about this scheme but he just pooh-poohed the whole thing.  Said he didn't give a damn what suited Phyllis and Terry – they'd never had any business sense.

A week later Nora rang. She was in a bit of a tizzy and I couldn't get a clear story out of her. She rarely rang us up, though to hear Geoffrey talk about it you'd think she was on to us every five minutes. I didn't want to tell Geoffrey about it and get him on his hobby horse again so I told him I was going to walk down to the hairdresser's. I don't think Geoffrey would have noticed if I'd had my head shaved and had rude words tattooed on my skull, he's that unobservant.

Nora was upset because one of her cats had died. She'd had him fourteen years, not a bad innings. But she'd had a shock: tapped him to get him off the ironing board and he was rigid. She couldn't bring herself to put him out with the rubbish and she'd no garden, just a tub outside with a conifer in and she could hardly bury him in that. I told her I'd take him and put him in our border.

I made us some tea and we had a chat and she calmed down.

The place was a bit of a tip; everywhere thick with cat hairs and ashtrays full of cigarette ends but it wasn't dirty. The cats were trained and she still managed to clean out their trays often enough. She'd seven of them left. Not counting Elvis who was now wrapped in a thick bin liner, in a shopping bag by the front door.

We'd never been all that close, Nora and I. It wasn't really possible with Geoffrey daggers drawn. He'd made it clear once we were hitched, that his mother was a cross to bear and the less we saw of her the better. But on the odd occasion that she and I got together it wasn't so bad, she was never funny with me. Geoffrey claimed you couldn't hold a decent conversation with her and that she was half-crazy but

I never saw that.

Walking back home I felt like I was carrying a weight with me – and I don't mean the cat.  There we were, me and Geoffrey, big house, big car, big garden.  Big and empty.  No cats, no kids, not even a goldfish.  Got me down, thinking that.

'Look at this.'  He passed me a brochure.  'Palm Beach View.  Paignton.'

'What's this?'

'A holiday,' he smiled.  'Good job you had your hair done.'

'We can't afford . . .'

'We can,' he had a funny look on his face, like he was building up to a surprise.  'Just a week.'

So we hadn't won the Lottery then.

'Me, you, my mother.'

'Nora!'

'She deserves a break.'

I realised then.  My stomach went cold.

'Geoffrey . . .'

'Shh!'  He put his fingers to his lips as if I were a child.  'It's all arranged.'

'But Nora – she might not want . . . there's her cats.'

'She'll go.'

And she did.  He rang her up and told her to sort out someone to feed the animals.  He was false jovial, if you get my drift.  'I want to treat the pair of you,' he said, 'you and Pamela.  And besides there's a third off next week.'  Which sounded more like it.

Nora probably thought I'd told him about Elvis and he wanted to cheer her up.  As it was, he'd been out at the travel agent's when I got back and I'd dug the creature a grave near the tea roses.

My stomach was upset so I just did omelettes that night. That was Tuesday. We were leaving on the Saturday. He kept quiet about it for the next day or two and I . . . well, I know it sounds pathetic but I was too frightened to ask.

Then he brings it up right in the middle of *Coronation Street*. He always does that, he knows it's the one programme I hate to miss. If I tried to breathe a word when he was watching one of his precious documentaries I'd soon know about it.

'It has to be an accident.'

'Geoffrey, I don't want to know.'

He stared at me then, over the top of his glasses. I felt close to tears and I knew that wouldn't impress him. I sniffed.

'Oh, pull yourself together,' he raised his voice. 'It's our only option.'

'No!'

'Pamela, I know what's best. Trust me.'

'I don't want to know.' I put my hands over my ears and closed my eyes. I felt him stride out of the room and slam the door.

'You look a bit peaky, love,' Nora said when we picked her up from home. 'Sea air'll do you the world of good.'

Geoffrey kept the radio on which saved us from having to make conversation. Now and again Nora would join in with some tune she liked, humming along and Geoffrey would switch to another programme.

The guest house was very nice. 'Ooh, look!' Nora cried when she saw the view from her room: the sea a petrol blue and the headland sweeping round. Her eyes were shining. 'It's perfect,' she turned and smiled at me.

I could feel a headache coming on as I unpacked but I didn't like to lie down and leave the two of them on their own.

The Sunday we drove round the district. We had a seafood lunch in Shaldon and then Geoffrey drove us right up to Dartmoor, where we saw the ponies, and back along by the River Dart. All the time it was like I was holding my breath, waiting for something to happen. Nora noticed. That evening when we went down to dinner Geoffrey had forgotten his sweeteners and went back up to fetch them.

'Everything all right?' she said. 'You don't seem so bright.'

I shrugged. 'Bit of a bad head.'

'This,' she nodded at our surroundings, she shook her head. 'Thank you.' She stretched out her hand and squeezed mine.

Oh, God. She thought it was my idea. That I'd wanted to treat her.


Monday we went up to Berry Head. It was fine weather, breezy on the top with blue skies, warm sunshine.

'Look at that,' Nora said, 'see half-way to France.'

'Have a stroll?' Geoffrey suggested.

I swallowed hard. There was a burning in my chest and my ears were buzzing.

'Lovely,' cooed Nora and she got out of the car.

I hesitated. 'My headache . . .'

'Nonsense,' Geoffrey said quickly, 'fresh air's just the job.'

The path was worn; the earth red like it is in Devon. White rocks were placed every few feet, to mark the path in poor weather. The shiny turf was dotted with daisies and clover. The cooler air carried the bitter tang of the grass and I fancied I could smell the brine from the sea. I caught the chirping sound of grasshoppers, saw one go flying off as we passed by. We don't get them round our way, not warm enough.

Geoffrey led the way, then me, then Nora. There were signs up: warning notices about the cliff and some sections were fenced off.

Eventually Geoffrey stopped and we followed suit. Three of us stood in a row looking out to sea. The land fell away only a yard or so in front of us.

Nora shielded her eyes and studied the horizon. I looked down at my shoes, I could feel my heart stuttering, missing a step. My mouth was dry. I glanced at Geoffrey and he winked *winked* at me.

'Look,' I said to Nora, my voice high, pointing away to my left, along the coast beyond her. And she turned to see.

I swung round and shoved with all my strength. I heard Nora cry out and I took a step forward to see the body bounce, once against the cliff side, then again on the jagged rocks, and land slumped like a puppet where the waves broke against the slabs of stone.

'Geoffrey!' I screamed, moving forwards and going down on my knees. 'Geoffrey!' The wind took my screams and flung them to the gulls.

'Oh, God!' Nora gasped.

'He slipped.' I was shaking, tears pricked in my eyes. 'That rock,' I pointed to the smooth boulder. 'I tried to catch him.'

She nodded, 'I saw you move.'

'Too late. Ambulance.' I staggered to my feet. I pulled my mobile phone out of my handbag. 'We never should have come. He said he felt dizzy this morning.' I pressed nine nine nine. The coastguards were very quick.

133

I sold the house. Too big for me, like a pea in a biscuit tin. I was going to get a flat somewhere that would suit if I needed help in years to come. Then Nora admitted the stairs at hers were getting too much for her and she was wondering about a bungalow.

It was a programme on telly set me thinking. And we ended up here – the Spanish Riviera. Geoffrey's life-insurance policy paid out more than enough. Turned out Nora had cashed hers in years back to make sure Geoffrey had everything he needed at school and could go to college.

We're tucked away on a little unmade road a few miles from the main drag. We've our own bit of beach out the back and the only other way to reach it is by sea. No one bothers – it's not even marked on the tourist maps. Nora's out there now, I can see her, cooling off, waist deep, fag in hand. The cats love it; basking in the sun and chasing lizards.

We've enough space for friends to visit, Phyllis and Terry are due on Sunday, and there's even Bingo, once a week, up in town. Bit of an expat enclave, really.

I've given a lot of things up: knitting and cooking and cleaning. We've a girl comes in, nice girl.

I read and I swim and I sleep like a baby. Nora has a telly in her lounge, gets everything on satellite, but I don't miss it. I'm learning the language and I do a bit of voluntary work – English conversation with the local children – those that need a bit of extra coaching. Keeps me young.

My golden years, that's how I think of them. Ended up here by accident really. When I look in the mirror, I don't see a killer, just a few more wrinkles every day – and most of them are laughter lines.

# SUSANNAH MARSHALL
## Small Mysteries

I really should have been raised in America. It's where my heart lies, though I've never actually been. I get my fix of the place from television; satellite and all its glorious channels. I'm away from home with my job for stretches of time but you can bet, when I'm home, I'll be hunkered down in front of the TV with some cans of Bud tuned in to *Court TV*, or *America's Most Wanted*. I do like to watch cop shows, or true crime, and when I can, I catch those shows that delve into the mind of a killer. America may be the land of the free, but it's also the land of the perps, the punks and the freaks. Still, I'd be happy to be counted as any one of these, just as long as I could call myself an American.

The guys at the depot are used to my ways by now. When I first started driving, they weren't too friendly: a chick, driving a truck. It's not like they could flirt with me either, I'd sooner have decked them, leaving them sparked out in the yard. They don't seem to mind my being around now. I don't really hang out with them but I'll have a bit of a banter with them in passing. They have nicknames for everyone here and I suppose the fact that they call me Yankee shows they've kinda accepted me.

I'm a driver for a haulage firm in Huddersfield. We specialise in hazardous-goods delivery. I personally drive an eighteen-tonne curtain-sider. I drive all round the country and across on the Continent, but being based in Huddersfield, I often drive up and down the M62. The M62 sure has its charms. I've grown quite fond of it. I don't even mind all the tailbacks and crazy drivers – the business-suited guys in their Audis and Mercs. Those jerks may have plenty of horsepower, but you can be sure they've also got small dicks. The jams are just about always on account of a smash. I'm a very careful driver, but it always sobers me when I pass by an accident. Rubber-necking is something I can't stand, and I get real mad at the drivers who slow down and scan the crumpled metal for a glimpse of blood and suffering. All I can think is some poor soul will not be going home to their families that night.

I've learnt from my time driving on the motorway that there are many small mysteries of the M62. For instance, it's guaranteed to be misty over Saddleworth Moor. Right at the place where you pass under the arching bridge that's so high it looks like it's in the clouds. At that point, you're on the highest motorway in Britain and fog is guaranteed. Bet your bottom dollar on it. I think that type of weather kinda suits Saddleworth. I used to get a chill when I passed by its rolling hills knowing that, somewhere out there are ghosts of children. I have no words for the likes of Brady and Hindley. In America, it would have been the electric chair for them. No question.

There are other mysteries too. Strangest thing I ever saw had to have been a couple of springtimes ago. I knew something was wrong because suddenly the free-flowing traffic in all three lanes began to slow. The M62's always busy and the volume of traffic meant we were crawling fender to fender for quite some way. I don't like to run late on a delivery, but sometimes you can't do anything about it. I just crank up the volume on the stereo in my cab and go with the flow. Country music's what I like most. Johnny Cash. Loretta Lynn. Tammy Wynette. Sometimes, I don't mind a bit of Elvis either.

After a mile or so, the dot matrix sign stated INCIDENT JCT 22 – 23 in flashing orange lights. 'Incident' is always a bit more mysterious than 'Accident'. The two should not be confused. I flicked the traffic info button on the stereo so my music would be interrupted at intervals by travel announcements. Before there was any news though, the dot matrix flashed up the symbol for two lanes closed, with just the inside lane remaining open.

In circumstances such as these, I can't help wondering what the incident might be. I have witnessed animals wandering on motorways before now. Usually, the lost fox or cat doesn't stand much chance with the speeding traffic. However, the stray cow or sheep can be much more problematic. Suicide is another possibility, especially when passing under bridges. I did hear on the grapevine at the depot that, years back, a guy gave up his job there because a jumper had once hit the front of his cab as he fell. I guess something like that must be kinda shocking. But I'd never give up my job driving trucks. I love it too much.

I'd gone about three or four miles by this point, and all the traffic started funnelling into one lane, herded by a diagonal line of cones. Although the traffic had been crawling before, it was almost at a standstill by now, on account of people rubber-necking as they passed the incident itself. The first thing I saw was a cop car parked up in the middle lane with its lights flashing, though no siren. The next thing I saw was a large pram sitting in the fast lane. It was one of those old-fashioned kinda ones; a perambulator with huge wheels full of spokes and a collapsible hood, like that one in the scene from the movie where it goes careering down some steps. With something so curious, I couldn't help taking a look as I passed by. A couple of cops in fluorescent yellow jackets stood near the pram. As I slowed and looked down from my cab into the raised hood, I saw a baby, laid there, fast asleep.

I never found out what happened. I thought it may have been on the news, but it wasn't. No one at the depot had heard anything either. I don't think the guys actually believed me. They probably thought it was something I'd imagined, on account of being a woman.

Occasionally, on long drives, particularly overnight ones, when I'm a bit weary and the miles of road pass by me in a reel like the backdrop in a fifties movie, the pram looms up on the horizon. The baby is awake and crying at these times. As the pram races toward me, the blackness of the baby's mouth grows and engulfs me, as though I'm driving into a tunnel. I know then it's time for a break.

I'm a regular at many of the services on the motorways of Britain, with their mugs of tea strong enough to support a teaspoon vertically like a flag-pole, and their rounds of toast yellow with margarine and curling at the crusts. I guess my truck and I are known to staff in some of these services by now. When I first started calling at services, many of the staff mistook me for a guy. This often happens to me, on account of my slender build and the way I dress, I suppose. I always wear my Wranglers and a chequered lumberjack kinda shirt. I generally wear a baseball cap too, pulled down to my brows. I've quite a collection of these, bearing the insignia of American baseball teams. The Red Sox, the Pittsburgh Pirates and the Blue Jays. I do have a pair of cowboy boots, but I don't usually wear these to drive my truck, just on special occasions. I've rigged out my cab with some American stuff. I've got a neon Budweiser sign that I can run off the engine. Sometimes I light it up if I'm night driving. I've got a Confederate flag too which is draped at the back of my cab. I'd love to get an American eagle airbrushed on the bodywork, but I don't think my employers would be too happy about that.

It was at a services, taking a break on a night drive, that I met Valentina. I was in need of a coffee to wake myself up. I was on a thirty-six-hour haul. Of course there are regulations now as to how long you can drive without a break, but sometimes these kinda get overlooked. A packet of Pro-plus and a few strong coffees can work wonders. I guess it was about two am, and the cafeteria was pretty much deserted. It was a big florescent hangar of a place with Formica tables and tubular steel. There was a couple of staff drifting about. A guy who looked like he could have been a student making a bit of money-propping himself up on a broom while he listlessly swept the floor, and a short woman, who I think was of Filipino descent, popping up every now and then from behind the counter. Other than that there was just me and one or two other customers. One was a middle-aged man who, though his clothes were smart, looked a bit dishevelled. His shirt was open at the collar, and his tie askew and loosened. His hair was messy and he had the beginnings of shadowed stubble on his chin. He looked to me like an over worked executive, returning from a business trip, or an illicit liaison with a mistress.

The other customer, I couldn't quite work out. She was a woman with long hair dyed bright orange and she was sitting with her legs drawn up, feet on the edge of the seat and knees pressed against her forehead. She had wrapped her arms across her knees and her hair draped across so I could not see her face.

In this kinda foetal position, she was rocking back and forward slightly. I could see that she had painted her nails with bottle-green varnish. I watched her while I drank my strong coffee. I thought maybe she was homeless and was seeking some shelter here at the services, or perhaps she was a prostitute working the motorways. It happens. Truckers and taxi drivers get lonely, same as businessmen.

Her rocking motion had evolved more into a kinda sway, as though she was listening to some music. I looked to see if she was wearing headphones. She wasn't, but at that moment, she raised her head. Her eyes were closed and I could see her mouth working. She was singing to herself. I wanted to be there, across the polished lino of the cafeteria, sitting close to her so I could hear the melody. Even feel the shape of the words against my cheek. She opened her eyes abruptly, green lizard-like eyes, snapping into focus to catch me staring.

I looked down into my mug of coffee, though I was sure she was still looking at me. She had caught me in those lizard sights of hers. I sipped at my coffee uneasily, looking anywhere but across the café in her direction. But when I next dared to take a quick look, she had got up and was walking toward my table. In those seconds between her leaving her table and crossing to mine, everything seemed to slow down, moving at an under water pace. I took in a lot of information in those moments. The girl was very tall, six foot or so, I would guess, and she was skinny. She wore bright clothes, a kinda jade-coloured silken skirt, lavender-coloured tights and black boots that looked like they belonged on a building site. She had on a fur jacket, purely silver as though it had come straight off the back of a wolf. Then she was sitting opposite me and her lips were as red as if she'd just bitten them.

I earn a fair wage in my job. I don't really have anyone to spend my money on, so I'm saving up and one day I want to make it to the States and drive a real big rig. One with all chrome exhausts and fenders, and banks of headlamps. I could start afresh in America. No one knows me there, and I can leave behind the whisperings of my past. It's all open roads too, straight as a die, stretching off into desert and prairie. And, there are far more folk hitching for rides in the US.

Valentina was hitching for a lift when I met her. It's pretty rare to find hitchers these days, particularly female ones. You do still get the occasional guy; sometimes a student, or another trucker who you can identify on account of their plates, which they hold out like a coded message. It's kinda trucking etiquette to pick up another driver if you see one, though I really don't like sharing my cab with guys. I never quite feel safe with them and besides, I don't like their smell, or the hair on the back of their hands. Gives me the creeps. That's why I couldn't believe it when Valentina asked me for a ride.

She sat opposite me at the Formica table, fixing me with her green eyes, and said, 'You will take me to London?' She spoke with some kinda accent, Russian I thought, and had that kinda brusque sound that foreigners have when they don't quite get phrases right.

I wasn't headed for London. I'd collected a load from the Borders and was supposed to be taking it down to Bristol and, at present, was just skirting Cumbria, but I looked right back at her from beneath the peak of my baseball cap and said, 'Sure, no problem.'

Originally, I planned on a kinda detour. Take the M6 down to Coventry, then pick up the M1 and take Valentina to London, before looping back on the M4 to Bristol. I guessed I'd hit London at rush hour, which wouldn't be good. I could maybe blame the delay on a burst tyre or something but, to be honest, I didn't give much of a shit about being late with the drop whilst Valentina was sitting there in my cab.

I'm not much of a talker, and that's partly why I like driving. It's just me and the road. Mile after mile of it. However, I did like Valentina, and was more than happy to sit by her taking in those miles while she talked to me. It didn't seem to matter to her that I didn't speak much. It was like she wanted someone just to be there to listen to what she said. And I did listen. To every single word, and each breath and hum of uncertainty she made when she wasn't quite sure if she was getting the language right.

'May I smoke?' she asked. I don't smoke myself, and normally wouldn't tolerate smoking in my cab, but Valentina could have just about taken out a knife and slashed the seats, or cracked the windscreen with one of the heavy silver rings she wore on her hand, and I wouldn't have minded. She rolled herself a thin cigarette from a packet of Golden Virginia. 'Your English tobacco is good,' she said. 'Polish tobacco, it is too bitter.' With the roll-up balanced on the edge of her lips, she leant forward and started to fiddle with the radio. 'You have good music too. In Poland, music is not good. Music is shit.' She laughed, briefly but with volume. She had tuned the radio to some pop station, something that usually I would avoid. Then she started to sway in her seat, as she had in the refectory when I first saw her. 'You like to dance?' she asked, without really waiting for a reply. 'I love to dance. Aurek, he did not like me to dance. In Poland, I must dance for money. I dance there at a club, and men, they pay money for it.'

I took my eyes off the road briefly to look at her. She was picking a fleck of tobacco from the tip of her tongue, still swaying to the music. 'Aurek, he does not know I am here. I must go to London and I will dance there.'

I broke my silence then. 'Who is Aurek?' I said. I turned my head quickly again for her response.

She caught my passing glance. 'My lover. Of course,' she said.

I swung my focus quickly back to the road. The Catseyes extinguished as the truck swallowed them.

'And you?' she said. 'You have a lover also?'

This time I kept my eyes on the road, but gave a scarce shrug of my shoulders. Valentina let out a quick burst of her voluminous laugh. 'You like to fuck girls?' she said, and laughed once more. Again, she didn't seem concerned about my response. She reached out to the radio, turned up the volume, then swung her legs up beneath her on the seat. She looked out of the side window then, and sang to herself quietly.

We were a good way through Cheshire at this point and would soon be crossing the Midlands. Valentina was quiet now, and the rhythm of her breathing told me she was sleeping. Just those constant but slight breaths soothed me. My cab was filled with her scent and her colour. If her eyes weren't closed in sleep, I would swear the cab had a faint luminescence borne from her green gaze. The M1 with its dawning rush hour and the goal of abandoning Valentina there at its end was doing nothing to lure me. Instead, Shropshire, with its maze of country roads, with darkness hovering over them longer, and leading into the solitude of Wales, had a stronger pull.

I guess I really wished I was in America then. Those miles of open road with not a soul around, except for me, Valentina and the odd turkey eagle flying way above.

It was not quite five am, and the traffic on the smaller roads was pretty scarce. From up in my cab, I could see the beam of headlamps on bright before any on coming vehicles there were got near enough to dip their lights. Valentina was sleeping soundly. The change of pace and noise on the smaller roads had not disturbed her. I had switched the racket of the pop station for the languid tones of Loretta Lynn and these seemed to act as a lullaby to Valentina. I saw the fork of a lay-by ahead and slowed the truck gently to a stop in it. It was one of those lay-bys that takes the form of a small arc of a lane, set back from the main road and divided off by bushes and trees.

The engine growled to a stillness. Valentina moved her head slightly and sucked in her bottom lip, but she did not wake up. I made sure the cab doors were on auto lock and unfastened my seat belt. I looked at Valentina. I took in every shape of her; the way she was curled somewhat awkwardly in the seat, like an untidy cat. I could have counted every thread of her hair if I'd wanted. I had no rush to go anywhere, and no one was around. I wanted to reach across and put my hand on her leg. I wanted to push the fabric of her skirt up to her thigh and slide my hand upward. I wanted to lick the stretch of her neck, exposed as her head tilted away from me, resting against the cab door in her sleep. I didn't do any of this. I didn't want to wake Valentina. If she woke up, we would have to hit the road once again. She'd want to know how far it was to London and when we'd be there. We'd soon find the company of other cars and trucks. She wouldn't be mine, in that moment, any longer. She'd choose those businessmen and their fat wallets in London's lap-dancing clubs over me, just as she'd chosen them over her boyfriend. I didn't want her to wake up. Ever.

I guess she really hadn't told Aurek where she'd gone. As the following days turned to weeks, no one seemed to note her absence and those seedy clubs in London didn't seem like they'd been waiting for her. Sometimes, when I've been driving for a stretch and I find myself getting tired, I do start to feel a bit anxious and play over her last moments. I start to sweat and shake and all I can see is those lizard eyes fixed on me, gradually filtering to red. That white exposed throat of hers is there in my hands like a cloth I'm wringing out. I guess time's running out for me on the English roads. I really need to be leaving for the highways of America. Land of promise.

# CHAR MARCH
## Will You Walk Into My Parlour?

They call me Ludmilla. Or Ludi, or Ludya, or Milla, or Lu-Lu. I let them choose their diminutive. For what are my feelings of distaste, compared to their need for intimacy with her? I like my ladies to feel ownership of her.

Over my kitchen table they whisper, chat, sob and giggle. Leaking out the secrets of their exclusive world. For Ludmilla is a good listener. Ready with just the right comforting phrase, just the right beverage for each, just the right toys to keep their brats quiet while each mother, nanny, girlfriend, babushka, Ukrainian au pair spills their beans. Ludmilla is always here for them; leaning forward with balm tissues for their red-rimmed eyes. I fine-tune her level of empathy; have her produce just the right chuckle to encourage their laughter. She is all things to all the women who scurry to my cosy parlour.

They make her just who they want her to be. She is motherly, or sisterly, or best friend, or wise counsellor, or stoic bulwark, or airhead chum, or stolid comrade. After all, it's important they feel thoroughly comfortable with her. I've found that always works best. I provide them with something – someone – they discover they've each wanted all along. Nothing wrong with that. In fact, it's a lovely thing to do, don't you think?

I take a pride in Ludmilla. She is complete customer satisfaction; the ultimate bespoke. An entirely un-Russian concept – even in the cut-throat kapitalisma of 2006 Moskva where everyone, just *everyone*, is trying to get the edge, the vital and elusive competitive edge. And where prioritising customer satisfaction is still as foreign as . . . politeness – which thus ensures my strategy is deliciously effective.

We've never had a single complaint. Not even afterwards. It's almost as if they truly believe she was worth it.

*

A description of Ludi – yes, you said you'd want one of those. Well, do you know, you're going to laugh, because . . . we just can't agree. It's strange – given the amount of time we each spend with her. Won't you have some Lapsang Souchong? Or do you prefer vodka – since it's afternoon? Nothing? Very well.

Start with something easy – like hair colour? Well, that's just it – Ruslana says Ludi's blonde; but Katya is adamant she's dark. Anna has plumped for curly; but Poppia says definitely long, and straight.

Ludi dresses . . . well, appropriate to her age. She's sort of comfortingly bland, we've decided, or, leastways, not bland, but not off-puttingly trendy. None of us have ever felt she's, you know, a rival in the fashion stakes. That's something we're all agreed on: we wouldn't feel concerned promenading down Tverskaya Ulitsa with her – we'd clearly not be out with a rival, but not out with a frump either. Not that any of us has ever walked anywhere with her – it turns out we've all just met her at her place. You see, Ludi acts as a great – what was that brilliant word you came up with, Natalya? – 'foil', that was it. Ludi acts as a great foil – to any of us. She shows us off at our best.

What exactly does she wear? Well, things a woman her age would wear. She's always so smart with me – all the latest Milan labels – but Yekaterina insists Ludi always wears some awful flowered housedress. Petra says tailored slacks – rather like hers. And on it goes.

Her age – well, it turns out we each feel she's *our* age, but, as you can see, that's a pretty broad band – Antonina, dear, how old are you? Fourteen? And I think Irena is our most . . . er . . . venerable lady. (Don't mind me whispering – she's deaf. You ought to know – for your own health: Irena's the daughter of Sergei Dzerzhinsky. Yes, everyone blenches like that. My husband gets so mad – can't understand why The Terror regime is still held in such . . . terror. Thinks his Vashchenko clan should strike a lot more . . . respect.)

Eighty-one did you say, Irena? You see, Ludi is just so comfortable to be with – you can't imagine, you've not been with her. Oh, you've got a form to fill in have you? Well then, maybe go for the average. Ha ha! That's a good one, Steffi – yes, our Ludi must be middle-aged if she's invisible!

Look, we want her back *much* more than you do – we miss her so much, but she'll be back soon.

Well, we just *know*.

There you go again – wanting details: what accent? What class? Where did she say she came from? You just don't get it – Ludi isn't like that. Ludi never says *anything* – about herself.

Oh, you find that suspicious do you? That shows what sort of mind you've got.

How did we meet Ludi? Well, the word just threaded its way out. You see, each of us liked to think Ludi was *our* little secret, but, I'm afraid we've all ended up just *having* to tell at least one other person. And Ludi's network just grew and grew.

Does she work? We've no idea, no one ever thought to ask. Tatiana? Oh, yes – perhaps our miraculous Ludi is head of a Duma-sponsored scheme to create more harmonious communities! Ha ha! Well, she certainly deserves a Soviet Woman of Honour and Courage medal, because she's done an excellent job around here. As you can hear from the hurrahs, my young comrade, the other ladies definitely agree. Ludi casts a shimmering web of comfort – and draws us all that bit closer, to ourselves, to her, to each other in a strange sort of way – even though we so very rarely meet each other.

How dare you ask if we give her money! Ludi is our friend – not some service we pay for!

Well, yes, our bank accounts have . . . gone down. But our menfolk – well, they like to move their assets around at short notice. Arilya? Yes, of course – they'll have sent it to off-shore investments or some such. We don't pay much attention to the day-to-day stuff. And since so many of our men have . . . er . . . left recently, well . . .

All right – disappeared, if you insist.

Yes, we know some of them have been murdered. Rivalries in our . . . business – well, they are commonplace.

Oh! Some of them say they're being blackmailed, eh? Well, and I bet my own son is amongst them – he always had an imagination, that good-for-nothing. Men just hate paying up, don't they? Any excuse – they'll say they're being blackmailed by the Party, by the oligarchs, by their ex-wives, by their mistresses. How are they ever going to live it down – they've gone into hiding because of some woman? If you believe that one, my fine comrade, you'll believe anything – it'll be some scam of their own, a tax dodge, or a contract that's backfired, or a territory war and they need to lie low for a while. We womenfolk are always the last to know.

Can't you leave poor Ludi alone? We don't know where she's gone. A well-earned break to the Black Sea; to look after an elderly aunt in Novosibirsk. When she gets back you can ask her yourself. And you'll be able to explain what you're doing to her lovely house and garden too!

How do *we* meet? We don't. We never even knew each other existed really – well, only by our husbands', our sons' . . . reputations – until a week ago. Yes, about a week after Ludi had gone off on her trip to wherever.

Obviously you have no experience of our sort of lifestyle – our neighbourhood *is* Moscow's first, of course. You'll still be living cheek-by-jowl with your neighbours in some dreadful rabbit-hutch the communists called People's Grand Living Apartments – with their filthy communal bins, and backyard bitching over the single washing line. Ah, I see I've struck a sore spot with you – Comrade.

It must be such a strange concept for you to grasp – here, we never see our neighbours. Privacy (such a lovely word) is one of the many privileges of capitalism. Inside each of our compounds – behind our security walls, our electronic gates, our bodyguards – we have everything we want. Or we order it in. That's right, Uyla – if we want to shop, Milan and Paris are just a couple of hours off – our private hangars at Sheremetyevo are only fifteen minutes' drive. 'Chi-chi Gulag', call it what you will. Yes, I heard you sniggering with your driver – the microphones at my entry gates are very powerful. But we have absolutely everything we want, despite Moscow still being so dreadfully . . . Russian.

Well, yes, everything except for Ludi. Ludi is well worth venturing out for. Do you know, I think she's the only other woman I've got to know – who's not in our clan, I mean. Oh, it's the same for you, Masha? – and you, Lineta? And Eliena? And . . . okay, thank you, ladies. Rather a chorus there, it seems. As you can hear, we like to keep ourselves to ourselves in this . . . neighbourhood. And besides, as you might be able to imagine, our menfolk prefer it that way.

Occasionally we'd spot each other – when we were on our way to Ludi's. Once or twice I'd be scurrying up Ludi's driveway as another of us floated beatifically down it – soothed and straightened out. But as soon as I am inside, I am Ludi's whole focus. 'Now, dear, tell me all about *you*.'

And she pulls up my favourite chair and makes me cappuccino exactly how I love it – with three muscovado sugars and . . . What, Marta? Oh, for you she makes perfect iced apple juice. How . . . healthy. You slosh back vodka-Martinis with Ludi, Ilyevna? But Ludi doesn't drink. No, no – Ludi's always been vehement about that. Well, she knows about my Boris's problem, and . . . Tequila slammers, Irena? At your age? But Ludi . . . she's always so anti-drink . . . with me.

What? Oh, well then she gives me the most marvellous foot massage. Particularly if I'm worn out with Bo-Bo's horde of kids. An Indian head massage, Valentina? – how wonderfully exotic! Shiatsu with you, Urenya? What's that? Oh, I see. It sounds rather rough. But on me, Ludi has the loveliest touch – she draws all these sticky threads of tension out. And she has the prettiest little parlour – it just seems to reach out and *hug* you. Well, until *you lot* got there and started tearing it apart – and all those huge men in white overall things digging up her lovely garden – she's going to be devastated when she gets back!

Why are we so convinced she'll be back? What

on earth do you mean?  You haven't got awful news have you?  Is Ludi . . . hurt?  You haven't hurt her have you?

Oh, that's a *huge* relief.

Aren't you taking notes in that silly little book of yours?  Watch my lips, my fresh-faced young officer: Ludmilla Paookova is coming back, because she loves us.

The money, the money, the money – we knew you'd be back to that.  Ludi has *nothing* to do with our money – it's complete coincidence.  You're just making ridiculous allegations, crazy assumptions.  It's typical of you apparatchiks to be so lazy – not even bothering to *try* to do your job properly.  Just because your wages have been cut, you think you can get away with any old rubbish.  Well, we pay our taxes – or some of us do – and we know our rights.  Yes, *rights* – a new concept in our Motherland – especially for you boys in uniform.  You should be out searching for the real villains who emptied our bank accounts.  Anyway, what evidence have you got that points at Ludi? – none!  Absolutely none, that's how much!

Anything else we can tell you about Ludi? – well, let's try to convince you once again: Ludi is a force for *good*.  In fact, we're only just starting to find out quite *how* much she's done for us.  Since she's not been around this past fortnight, we've turned to each other.  It's nowhere near a replacement for Ludi, of course.  But it's been nice – swopping our different stories of how Ludi has helped us.  Take poor old Mishkya – she poured out to Ludi about Dimitri still hitting her after nearly sixty years of married 'bliss', and just the next week – his nasty fall.   And Liyania here giving birth to her little girl at home and the midwife making such a mess of it all – drunk she was!  See what I said about you state workers?

I always use the American private health clinic in Katinska quarter, but Liyania's boyfriend had only moved her here from that lap-dance bar in Minsk the month before – so she didn't know the ropes. Her little Elize will never be right you know – and then, just a few days after, there was that pile-up between the two ambulances – and no more midwife.

Oh, thank you, Mileva – you're quite right, we *did* decide not to discuss any of our, er . . . silly coincidences. But – do you know – the more we women have talked together it's funny how many tales we've each got of . . . anyway, officer, we shouldn't keep you – you should be out there beating up Chechens. Not sitting here listening to a bunch of women chat on about their best *bubeleh*.

Ludi's sewing? Well, she sewed each of our neck-charms . . .

Oh, the wall panel – all those beautiful tiny stitches. Ludi's been embroidering that since I met her.

Five months, you say? That's all she's been here? Amazing – I feel I've known her my entire life.

She said the wall panel was a comforting homily by Dostoevsky. I thought he just wrote gloomy stuff, but Ludi said no, this was heart-warming. Can you read it yet? – she's doing it in so many different colours, she said the writing would only swim to the surface at the last minute. Oh, all right – we'll see it when you've finished. What else is there?

Will you *stop* going on about the money?! No, of course we never gave out our bank details to anyone – what do you think we are – gullible? Look, there's no need to be coy, Comrade Detective, you know who all our husbands, our sons are – do you really think we'll run short?!

Oh yes, thank you for reminding me, Ankela –

we'd all like our neck-charms back now. We know you said they were vital evidence, but, they're just silly little gingham bags of herby bits and bats. It's not that they're important, but, well, we've got a bit superstitious about them – they're our lucky charms. Ludi gave us them, and you know what women are like about little sentimental keepsakes.

You need to retain them for another few *months*?!! Oh goodness! Now, ladies – now, now! Pleeeease! You did elect me as your spokesperson, and you did all agree not to speak at once. However, I believe – and hope – that that was a valuable insight for our young officer on our strength of feeling.

They're ours! They're personal! They're none of your damn business! Is that enough reasons for you?! We need them . . .

Well, no, of course I don't mean we *need* them – not like that. We just *like* them – yes, that's it. They're ours and we have a right to them and our best friend gave them to us as a little sort of pick-me-up, a little treat, a little . . . Look, just give us them back, eh?

Oh, puleeeease Detective Comrade, they're itsy bits of handicraft, we never thought much of them really, but it made her happy that we wore them – she always checks we've still got them on. Said they'd sort out insomnia, 'keep them on at night, sweeties' she said, and gosh, didn't we all sleep well! I've barely had a wink since you took mine away.

Ooooo, you've had them analysed – well, who's a clever boy then? No, we don't want to know what's in them. They're keepsakes with a bit of this and that out of Ludi's herb garden in . . .

Concentrated psychotropic what? But Ludi's . . . No – it's just not true. Ladies – please, please! Quiet! . . . Ha! Yes, you're quite right, Alexya – we *do* all know how much the police adore planting drugs. Yes ... yes, that's it.

Ludi gave them to us for luck, and look what's happened since you took them away – our darling Ludi has disappeared and some crook has emptied our bank accounts.

Yes, all right, and most of our cars have been stolen – that'll be gangs coming out here from some vile area like Novaya Brzinsk.

A convoy of transporters were used? But ... but that takes organising. This is starting to sound like ... like a job. So, where are they now?

They've crossed the Polish border? Well – get them back!

How do you *lose* a convoy of transporters?

Our money being moved out, the transporters ... Boris! He can still organise – they all can – from inside. You've no idea what it was like living with them. It was Ludi helped us get so many of the violent bastards put away. What, Katya? Yes, pinning the nightclub murders on your Vladimir was brilliant. Ladies, please! I know, I know – if those bastards think they can get away with revenge on us ... Quite right, Natalya – *we* run things now! Yes, Irena, we should have taken out more contracts on them – like Ludi said.

Well? What are you still doing here? Get out there and stop them! Oh, for goodness' sake – another revelation about Ludi? Well – what is it?

---

I wanted to murder, for my own satisfaction ....
At that moment I did not care a damn
whether I would become the benefactor of someone,
or would spend the rest of my life like a spider
catching them all in my web
and sucking the living juices out of them.
*Fyodor Dostoevsky*

*

You really shouldn't believe everything you hear.

Those Moscow Mafia women, they're hardly a sweet and innocent bunch. Why believe them? The police aren't at all convinced. After all, the women weren't even able to come up with a coherent description of Ludmilla.

All the women have been taken into custody. Implicated in all sorts of crimes; some anonymous tip-off with a mass of detailed information.

Oh, you think that must have come from Ludmilla? Haven't you considered the husbands and sons they betrayed? The ones now in hiding, knowing their wife, their mother had a contract taken out on them; the ones now in jail because of evidence from their mistress, their sister. Are you saying the men aren't going to want vengeance?

Those pampered nouveau-riche women, the ones it is so easy to despise; they aren't stupid. They could have got their act together; have spun the idea of Ludmilla; woven the logistics of her. Threaded her together in a complex weave over their scared conversations, while they held ice-bags against their latest black eye, their latest kicked belly. They have all the know-how – gleaned from their men: how to set up a contract on someone; how to take over a territory.

And who is to say that they won't pull it off? For the only thing that calls the shots in Moscow now is big money. And they still have control of vast webs of money. For, even if Ludmilla did exist, she only stripped current assets: the 'trades' are still intact – the sex-trade, the drugs, the people-trafficking – still pouring billions of roubles in every week. The women's jewel-heavy fingers can haul in nets of it whenever they want – with obliging police and judges and Duma members attached.

Now you're not quite sure – are you? And neither are the women, or their menfolk, or the police. They are all caught in sticky threads of doubt – cocooned in it. They are so busy following all the various threads, it will take them some time to realise they're going round in circles.

It's such an old trick: divide and rule. But it works every time.

I'll let you in on a secret: always pick on someone who everyone else would love to see take a fall. Oh, you thought I hit on the mafia wives because of my strong sense of right and wrong? Tell me – who else in God-awful Russia has any damn money to take?

Would you care for a cocktail? No? Oh, I find they are delicious to sip – particularly in this heat. I'm just getting used to it – I've booked in here for a couple of months. I hear it's popular with . . . well, my next customers.

# SUZANNE ELVIDGE

## Widows

'I understand you are another widow. So, what was your husband's name?' She slid a cigarette out of a crumpled packet with a long, burgundy nail, her ringless hands still graceful. She pushed the pack over to me across the table, lighting her cigarette with a disposable lighter that she handled as if it was a thing of value.

I took one, savouring the fresh damp smell of the fragrant tobacco. She leaned across and lit it for me, and I breathed in deeply, holding the smoke in my lungs for a moment before letting it out with a sigh. It had been so long that the hit of the nicotine made me feel dizzy.

'So?' I realised she was looking at me, still expecting an answer. 'His name?'

'His name? Oh yes.' I shook my head to clear it and tapped the white tail of ash into the ashtray. The smoke swirled up around us, and I waved my hand to clear it.

'His name was Kurt.' I took another drag of the cigarette and my head swam again. I placed the half-smoked cigarette in the ashtray, and propped my elbows on the cheap, scarred wooden table-top, resting my chin on my folded hands.

'Well, my dear, you are the youngest and prettiest to join us,' she said and patted my hand sympathetically. 'What happened to him?'

I smiled a wistful, gentle smile and took a moment to untwist my hair and knot it back, skewering the tortoiseshell comb through to secure it. 'He died making love.' I picked up the cigarette, gazing into the dull red glow, watching the tobacco flakes burn up into ash.

'What a sweet way to go.' My companion patted my hand again, and I laughed, stubbing my cigarette out, stabbing it into the bottom of the shallow plastic ashtray, warped and discoloured from so many years of use. 1-2-3-4-5-6-7-8. Until it had really gone out. As the sparks died, she clutched my hand until her swollen knuckles whitened.

'It would have been sweet if he had been making love to me. But at least he shared his final moments, I suppose.' I patted her hand as she let mine go, and eased my fingers out discretely where her strong grip had stopped the flow of blood. 'How did you lose your husband?'

'Marcelo? Sadly, he ate something that disagreed with him. It was just after he disagreed with me.' She toyed with her lighter, flicking it and making it spark.

'Oh, I am sorry. Maybe it was an intolerance?' I said.

She finished her drink, tipping it up to catch the last few drops, and then, suddenly, clenched her fist around the fragile tumbler. I jumped as the plastic shattered with a retort like a gunshot, and a bright bead of blood welled up on the tip of her finger. She licked the blood off slowly, almost thoughtfully.

'Mmm, I think that maybe it was. Intolerance to something anyway.' She brushed the shards away and lit another cigarette, the glowing tip burning bright crimson in the low light as she inhaled.

'I assume that you ate something different?' I asked, picking up one of the splinters of plastic that she had missed, playing with it, tracing the small white half-moon scars on my palm and pressing the sharp tip into the fleshy base of my thumb until the soft tissue whitened.

'Oh yes,' she said and smiled, and her face was all at once joyful and saturnine, and very, very young. I couldn't bear to meet the secrets in her grey eyes and looked at my tumbler, tracing a drop of condensation down its side with my finger, following it down to the table where it pooled at the base, the wetness staining the pale unvarnished wood a dark red.

We sat in quiet consideration for a moment, each in our own thoughts. She took a breath as if to speak, and then we heard last call over the speakers, crackling and near and distant. I drained my drink, the tang of the lemonade making me ache for the cut of vodka, the bell tones of ice on glass and the sharp brightness of biting into a slice of real lemon, alcohol-drenched and cold.

She tucked the cigarettes and lighter into her pocket and we headed back to our single rooms down the long corridors, past the watchful eyes and serried rows of doors.

Once in my room, the door closed itself and I heard the automatic lock click into place. I looked ruefully at the back of the handleless door and my hands closed tight into fists. I opened them slowly and looked at the eight moon-shaped crimson marks, four on each pale palm.

I'd been quietly preparing supper in the kitchen when I'd heard them come in, saw them come through the door, reflected in the shiny surface of the polished steel microwave.

I saw him undress her, heard the silken rustle of her scarlet dress as I sliced into the onions, brushing their papery red skins onto the work surface.

Watched his hungry eyes and grasping hands as I chopped the jalapenos, shredded the pink-skinned garlic.

161

Saw her back arch as he thrust into her, her legs wrapped around his as I slid the Camargue red rice smoothly into the seething water.

Smelt the rich raw smell of sex as I crushed the plum tomatoes, pips and juice sliding yellow and red beneath my fingers.

Heard her cries of climax and his grunts of satisfaction as the red kidney beans boiled over, the cherry-red-tinged froth splashing on the terracotta-tiled floor.

Felt the solidity of the knife in my hand, as I cut the tender fat-threaded steak into thin strips and slid them into the sizzling olive oil in the heavy iron skillet.

Gripped the handle until my nails cut into my palms, flecks of raw red beef still on the blade.

Felt the drumbeat of blood in my head.

1-2-3-4-5-6-7-8.

And then the noises stopped.

And I tasted his blood and hers splattered on my lips.

Salt and bitter.

And sweet.

# MAYA CHOWDHRY
## Acting Real

*Welcome to the world of the three Xs,*
*welcome to my world.*
*One2one pages, you can bi,*
*you can try,*
*welcome one and all.*
*Power tools and tampons,*
*Pepsi and Nike, I'll force you to look,*
*and next time you go for a six-pack*
*I'll be your branded sex-pack.*
*You're no perverted purchaser of porn,*
*a humble consumer operating erotic deals*
*from your remote-controlled sofa.*

Lexy, twenty-eight, ochre skin, wearing a short purple denim skirt, fish-net tights, a black wig, a cropped pussy-lick T-shirt and pin-striped jacket, swings her hips, stares the director straight in his eyes and then totters stage-right.

MIX TO: It is dusk; the sun sets slowly at the end of Sackville Street, sends red light across the clouds and down the side of the brick buildings. Lexy stands in the shadows looking at the city-worn winter branches against the sky, suddenly she leaps out, marches across the road and disappears up a narrow alley.

She chunters to herself, 'I don't want it anyway, it's a shit play, yes I do, I could make it mine, it'll be a laugh, get me off the dole, the agency's about to chuck me off the books, I could sell the house out!' Lexy turns the corner, Cassie's Cock-Tales beams out in neon red above the door, she crosses the road and strides in. Lexy hauls herself up on a bar stool and stares straight ahead.

'You didn't get it?' Cassie polishes a long-fluted cocktail glass, eyes fixed on Lexy.

'Who knows? Who cares? I do.'

Cassie fixes Lexy and herself a tequila slammer, pulls up a stool next to her and swivels Lexy round to face her. Lexy drags herself off the stool and ambles over to the jukebox, she selects without looking up the number. Patti Smith's *Gloria* blares out. The women look at each other, Lexy almost smiles, they lick salt, down the drinks, suck lime and Cassie returns behind the bar and starts making a margarita. Lexy gets up, 'I gotta go babe.'

Cassie looks in Lexy's face for a reason, but it's hidden so she picks up the free paper and starts to scan it. Lexy leans over the bar waiting for Cassie to kiss her, in the waiting moment she's distracted by an advert in the Wanted section in the paper in front of her. Without looking up Cassie leans over to kiss Lexy but she's engrossed, Cassie plonks a wet kiss on Lexy's nose. Lexy grabs the paper from Cassie, strides out of the bar and into the dusk of the street.

Earn £10,000 per week, if you're good enough! Women's Passion Emporium seeks star sellers for retail adventure. Call Kellyn on 0777 666 123.

'One, two, three. She'll do very nicely!'

There's a large crimson chandelier gracing the centre of the ceiling decorating the corners of the lobby with fractured light. Lexy is draped on a maroon sofa wearing her audition outfit, she reaches into the inner pocket of her jacket and clicks the on-switch on her

Dictaphone; it whirs into action.

CUT TO: Interior, Sackville Hotel. Lexy spies a woman, thirties, wearing a man's suit, stiletto heels and carrying a briefcase, as she marches across the imitation marble lobby. Their eyes meet, lock into a gaze and then release.

Kellyn stretches her hand out to greet Lexy aka Jez E Bell, who remains seated. 'Jez, I'm so sorry, my flight was late.'

Jez extends her hand slightly, but not enough for Kellyn to reach, Kellyn leans forward displaying a cleavage of firm rounded breasts encapsulated in an ivory pseudo-bodice. Jez's hand goes limp and then she regains composure and shakes Kellyn's hand firmly, gazing into her hazel eyes.

'Great to finally see the real you after all those phone calls and faxes.' Jez gestures for Kellyn to sit opposite her as if Jez was welcoming her into her own living room.

The stage is set. The drama has begun with a scene.

PROLOGUE: Lexy sits in her dressing room at the Theatre on the Canal; the walls are painted cerise with a motif of gold roses. She perches on the edge of a swivel chair opposite an ornate oriental mirror; she massages her cheeks and pouts her lips. 'I need to get into her blood stream, become one of her cells with the memory of her whole life encoded, absorb her by osmosis until her reality becomes mine.'

CHARACTERS:
Lexy: twenty-eight, ochre skin, wearing a short purple denim skirt, fish-net

tights, a black wig, a cropped pussy-
lick T-shirt and pin-striped jacket.
Kellyn: thirties, wearing a man's suit,
stiletto heels and carrying a briefcase.
Jezebel: character in Sex Sells.
Jez E Bell: Lexy's pseudonym.

FADE UP: SCENE 1: Sackville Hotel, Jez poised,
Kellyn staring carnivorously at her. 'Shall I run
through the details again?'

'No, it's quite clear, did you bring the proposal
and catalogue?' Jez tries not to grin.

Kellyn takes a catalogue from her briefcase and
lays it on the table, there's a photograph of a woman
in a G-string and tattoos lying amongst cactuses on
the front. Kellyn's eyes are fixed on Jez, searching for
a reaction. Jez coolly reaches out for the catalogue
and flicks through it delightedly. 'Fantastic! What a
sumptuous range.'

'You said you were an actress,' Kellyn probes.

'Yes, but you have to have your fingers in other
pies, it doesn't always pay the rent.'

'No mortgage then?' Kellyn seizes the chance to
check out Jez's financial position.

'Actor not film-star!' Jez laughs, bit of a fake
laugh which she curtails before she appears false.

'But will you have enough time to set up the
franchise?'

'Of course! I'm researching a part that I've
auditioned for, I haven't heard back, but if you'll have
me on board I won't need to act.' Jez looks straight at
Kellyn unflinchingly.

'I like your poise, your manner, appearance,
everything is totally right.' Kellyn lures.

Jez turns over a page and reads, 'You can't
measure a woman's pleasure!'

'I usually suggest trying out some of our products and developing your own sales pitch. Any questions?' Kellyn hands Jez some forms for her to complete. 'It's clear from your CV and references that you're an old hand at Network Marketing.'

Jez dumps these on the table without even glancing at them. 'I'm intrigued by how you started, where you got the idea from.'

'It's a bit of a personal tale, but I can tell you're trustworthy. It all started when my ex Richelle dumped me from a great height and after the bruises faded I wanted sex but couldn't trust anyone, I hadn't had an orgasm for three months, my chi was fading and I had no lust for life. I was on gaydar girls looking for a fantasy and inadvertently clicked into a world of lace and mock-cocks and thought I'd give myself a treat.'

Jez's gaze flicks from the hazel eyes to the ample bosom and back again as Kellyn recounts her tale. She realises, as Kellyn reaches the climax of the story, that she is becoming damp between her thighs and she can smell her aroma. She pulls herself back from predator to scrutiniser and continues to listen.

'Well, I won't go into the sordid detail,' Kellyn laughs hard. 'I built an international business from scratch and the rest is herstory.'

'Business and politics, I didn't think they mixed,' Lexy prods.

'Business is political, I don't see the division. Or between business and pleasure, art and business, tickets have to sell for your plays, and if they don't . . .'

'The show goes on regardless. I can't stand playing to half an auditorium, I don't feel appreciated.'

'And if it's not sold out it's the fault of the marketing department, not the artistic integrity?' Kellyn continues, enjoying making a theory up on the spot.

'That's a point, I'd never really thought of it like that, I can get fantastic reviews and still not sell out,' Lexy declares, trying to appear naive.

'Well I must dash, check me out, give me a call, here's my mobile.' Kellyn hands Jez her business card, it has a cheeky cartoon rabbit on it winking.

There are geraniums and begonias hanging entwined on the balcony, they reach down to a planter containing love-lies-bleeding which graces the steel-sculpted garden. Lexy sits at a round mosaic table, she flicks the switch on her Dick-tap-phone and scribbles into a notepad as Kellyn's voice recounts the afternoon's meeting; 'business is political . . .'

Lexy switches the voice off and stares at her notes, 'got it, got you.'

CUT TO: Lexy enters downstage, she fixes her gaze on the *Chairman Deluxe Office Massage Chair* centre stage; as she approaches she runs her hand along the top, somewhere between caressing it and dismissing it. 'Order, order, order and *I* have to submit, the order. Sell, sell, sell, self. Unique Selling Proposition, or is it Point? The point is to make money, or is it to make yourself?'

The director leaps off his seat and flings the script at Lexy, 'A, what's the point of rehearsal if you don't know your lines and B, you're supposed to be a businesswoman, not a call-girl. Take a coffee break and don't come back until you can give me what I want.'

MIX TO: The dressing room of the Theatre on the Canal. Lexy puts on her wig, and looks in the mirror, reads, 'Jezebel, proprietor of the establishment Sex

Sells sits on her balcony facing the western Manchester skyline swigging a double espresso.'

Lexy kicks the wall, swivels the chair, spins around three-hundred and sixty degrees and stares at her reflection, 'do I do yoga, t'ai chi, Pilates or keep-fit? Do I favour Mexican, Cantonese or Italian? Shop in the Northern Quarter or a retail outlet? Recycle or waste resources? Do I like to fuck or be fucked or both? Buy cut flowers or order online? Drink in the Village or Castlefield?'

She picks up her script and glances over the page and then dumps it down. 'Fickle? I call it having taste, being discerning, knowing what to have when and changing my mind accordingly.' Lexy opens her mouth wide, yawns and clicks her jaw. She scrunches her face into a point and then releases. 'Fickle? I call it having taste, being discerning, knowing what to have when and changing my mind accordingly.'

Standing under the house-lights in full costume, a mobile phone in each hand, Lexy looks across the bare stage diagonally into the empty auditorium, Lexy reads from the script: 'It is seven am Jezebel pours herself an espresso and sits down at the breakfast bar in her Sackville Studio. She glances at her watch; at that precise moment her mobile bleep bleeps the presence of a message. Jez replies and swigs on her coffee.' Lexy checks her phone for messages and then checks Jez E Bell's phone.

Lexy reads the text from Kellyn again, 'bad manners', she thinks to herself, 'to put money before pleasure, to discuss it via such a crude method of communication, open to misinterpretation. And, she never said money upfront.'

Lexy enters her studio apartment, she whips the wig

off and casts it to the ground, she stomps around the flat examining if there's anything to sell, but she knows there isn't. She rings the SM at the theatre and when she's rebuked she flings her mobile down, luckily it bounces off the wig and scoots along the wooden floor, stopping abruptly at the door. 'A risk! I'm the one taking the risk with this play, it's my arse on the line if the show's too *risqué*, it's my face on the posters, my naked body on stage with the audience stripping my flesh off until they can see my heart beating.'

MIX TO: Cassie's, Sackville Street. Kellyn, wearing a short blue silk skirt, sits opposite Jez on matching leatherette sofas, Madonna blares out. Kellyn stirs her drink uncomfortably. 'I can't imagine why anyone would want to drink in a place like this.'

'Some women like a bit of rough,' Jez grins.

Kellyn sucks her cocktail up through a straw, 'so what's this adventure you're taking me on?'

Jez moves across and sits next to Kellyn, 'close your eyes.'

Kellyn ponders, 'okay.'

Jez takes out some false eyelash glue, 'you're gonna feel me touch your eyelashes,' and she glues together Kellyn's lashes. 'Put these on,' Jez hands Kellyn a pair of dark sunglasses, 'and take my hand.'

Kellyn obliges with an enhanced confidence as if she half expects what's coming. Jez leads Kellyn out of the bar and walks her to the metro where she buys an all-day ticket and takes several rides back and to, through green-leafy suburbs and over bridges; alongside windy harbours and finally, when Jez knows Kellyn has lost all sense of direction, she leads her out of the tram, down the steps and alongside the canal.

MIX TO: the narrowboat creaks as it's pushed from side to side by the winter waves, blown first east and then west. Kellyn falters as she's led down into the boat; she hides her delight behind silence. Jez tries not to smile, even though she knows Kellyn is blind to her plan, as she sits Kellyn down on a wooden chair. Kellyn gasps as Jez handcuffs her to the chair, spreads her legs and ties her ankles to the legs of the chair, she can feel Jez's breath hot on her bare legs and feel velvet gloves brush her skin. Jez pulls on the square-lash knots to check their binding, she clips the key from the handcuffs to her keychain and marches elegantly out the cabin. She locks the padlock on the cabin and leaps off the narrowboat.

CUT TO: Lexy saunters down King Street towards Castlefield and stands in front of a large warehouse, she rummages through Kellyn's bag, finds a credit card statement and checks the address; 13 Canal View. Lexy enters the loft apartment and stands transfixed. There is a large chandelier dripping into the room, oak floorboards, pink walls and a kitchen to die for. She can hardly think amongst the opulence. She finds the bathroom, puts on her black wig, props a photograph of Kellyn beside the mirror and applies make-up from Kellyn's cabinet; scarlet lipstick, black eyeliner. 'Not bad, not bad at all.' Lexy swoops into the centre of the room, takes a deep breath and holds herself in a pose not unlike Kellyn's, the first time they met.

'I'll make you an offer you can't refuse, a perverted proposition.' Lexy sits down on a red velvet *chaise-longue* reading from the script of *Sex Sells*, 'bit of a cliché, don't you think?' She continues reading, 'thirteen years ago ninety two per cent of strap-ons were bought by lesbians, today over a third are snapped up by straight couples getting in on the silicone acts . . .'

Lexy slides back a large oak door revealing rails full of Kellyn's clothes, designer suits, cocktail dresses, rows of shoes. Lexy spies the suit Kellyn was wearing when they met, pulls it towards her, sniffs the crotch and smiles. She yanks it off the rail and it slides to the floor, hanging inside it is Kellyn's dildo and harness. Lexy tries on the suit as if she's having sex with Kellyn; slipping her hands inside and all over it, she zips up the fly and puts her hand on her mock-cock, 'perfect'.

Lexy clips a micro-video camera to her lapel and stalks the flat, inch by inch; she is drawn towards the drawers and boxes, to the revelations within, but no time. She takes mental notes and then shrieks with glee as she finds her prize. On the oak bookshelf, between *Blue Ocean Strategy: How to Create Uncontested Market Space and Make the Competition Irrelevant* and *Hardball Strategy: Are You Playing to Play or Playing to Win?* and stuffed in the back of *You Want It? You Got It!* by Mr McD, is Kellyn's passport.

Lexy parks Kellyn's car back in the car park of Cassie's, she retraces her steps to the canal side and enters the boat. She stands valiantly as Jez E Bell. Kellyn gasps and cocks her head towards the sound of Jez entering. Jez kneels in front of Kellyn and admires the scene. She licks Kellyn's ankles, slightly chafed from where she has been trying to struggle free. Kellyn is angry and excited, the afternoon not being entirely as she had fantasised it, she wants to speak but is hoarse from shouting this last half hour, having had a slight panic that she had been abandoned. Jez continues to lick, around her anklebones and up her legs until she is sucking the tender skin of Kellyn's inner thighs, she holds her with her gloved hands and dives tongue first into the place she has been imagining as Jez. Kellyn tilts herself, opening to Jez's mouth, tongue, to the spreading of her pussy and to Jez fucking her with her velvet gloved fingers. The boat tilts to one side knocking Jez off balance as she squats on Kellyn's foot, Jez thrusts herself forward and Kellyn can feel Jez's mock-cock. Jez tastes the moment of Kellyn's orgasm and stops fucking her, withdraws her mouth from around Kellyn's clit.

'Don't you stop now you bit . . .!' Kellyn chides.

'Patience is . . .' Jez retorts. 'There's the matter of consent.' Jez takes off the sunglasses and wipes Kellyn's eyes until they blink free. Jez is revealed wearing Kellyn's best Armani suit and sporting her finest dildo, Kellyn laughs out loud.

Jez has a clipboard, she reads from it, 'I Kellyn Bell give my whole consent to the play that is about to commence and confirm that my safe word is dot dot dot.' Jez undoes one of the handcuffs and passes Kellyn a pen and she signs eagerly, filling in the word *bread* on the dotted line. Jez admires her catch, pulls a scarlet fluffy blindfold from her pocket and strokes Kellyn's face with it. She ties it over Kellyn's eyes plummeting her into the dark fantasy she has signed up for. Jez begins to untie Kellyn's ankles. Kellyn is disappointed, wants to protest but she wants the scene to run out with her imagination so she allows Jez to continue. Jez hauls Kellyn to her feet and bends her over the chair.

Kellyn, face hidden, allows herself a smile, 'she's better than I thought,' she thinks to herself.

Jez slips the skirt from Kellyn's hips, admires her firm cheeks, runs her index finger over her G-string. Kellyn groans. Jez slaps each buttock until they are shiny red and Kellyn stops screaming 'harder'. Jez knows Kellyn wants her to fuck her; she can feel the tension in her body, her turned-on smell released from her cunt. But she must beg her to fuck her. Jez pushes against Kellyn's arse so the mock-cock rubs her crack, Kellyn groans. 'Please fuck me.'

'That's not begging,' Jez slaps and teases her in turn, pushes her legs wider, runs her fingers over her cunt, feeling its drenchedness through her G-string. She stops, leaves her breathless. Kellyn arches her back.

'Have I got the job?' Jez pushes the mock-cock deep into Kellyn's dripping pussy, Kellyn groans, 'we'll see,' Kellyn gasps, enjoying the candidate applying for the position. 'There's still the matter of the thousand pounds up front.'

Jez continues to fuck her; thrusting and twisting, holding her tight to her. Kellyn splutters, comes and Jez keeps fucking until she begs her to stop.

'Not until it's safe,' Jez commands and fucks her into the place where no means no.

Jez folds the consent form and puts it in her inside pocket and zips up her fly. She opens the door to the cabin, leaps from the boat and sashays along the canal side.

CUT TO: Interior, university office, there is a large oak desk in the corner of the room, strewn with papers, in the middle of the mess is a silver laptop and in front of that sits Akilah; late twenties, blue Mohican, ripped jeans and striped shirt. She taps the keyboard and sighs, rummages through the papers on the desk and continues typing.

Lexy barges in the room without knocking and Akilah jumps, looks up and closes the lid of the laptop. 'Can I help you?' she spits out.

Lexy smiles wryly, 'top secret?'

Akilah gets up, 'I didn't recognise you in that wig!' She goes over and kisses Lexy wetly on the lips, 'you know it is! I thought you were coming next week, how d'you get past security?'

'We've started rehearsal early,' Lexy flashes a university security card with her photo on it.

'How did . . . what you up to?'

Lexy perches on the edge of a seat, hitching up the tight skirt and revealing the place where the soft skin on her brown thighs meets. 'What d'you mean?'

Akilah sits down opposite her. 'Why did you go to the bother of making a fake ID card? Why didn't you just phone me from reception like you usually do?'

'Fancied testing out the security.'

'Well I should report this breach of security, if anyone . . .'

'Yeah, yeah, someone could get in and steal the crown jewels.'

'I'm serious, my whole . . .'

Lexy slips the ID card into her pocket, she interrupts and mimics Akilah in a seductive way, 'research is at stake.' Akilah glares at Lexy, who arches her back slightly and pushes her breasts forward. 'Keep your hair on, I'm just playing with you.'

Akilah's eye is caught and she momentarily loses herself in the place where breasts disappear from sight beneath red lace. 'I still don't understand why the props department at the theatre can't make them.'

'They can, but it'll look crap, not real. I want everything to be perfect.'

'What you got then?'

'Passport, driving licence and credit card statement, and some photos of me as Jez . . . I mean Kellyn Bell.' Lexy dumps the documents on Akilah's lap.

'I shouldn't really be doing this; I think it might be illegal, I could get sacked. Whose documents are . . .?'

'It's not illegal, it's art,' Lexy coos.

'Yes, but what I'm about to do is science.'

'Is it?' Lexy plays with Akilah.

'You know damn well it is; now stop flirting and let me get on with my work.'

'Can't we go for lunch? My treat,' Lexy exclaims.

'No, because you know what'll happen.'

'I'll drop my napkin and slip under the starched white table-cloth.'

'And while I'm slipping oysters down my throat . . .'

'I'll be slipping . . .'

'Don't say another word!' Akilah cuts her off before she's seduced into procrastination.

'Did you know that fifty per cent of UK women now own a sex toy? That's a very large market to exploit.'

'Is that a line from your new play?'

Lexy shrugs her shoulders, 'don't want to ruin the opening for you.' She thrusts a flyer for the play into Akilah's hand.

'Eighty per cent of statistics are made up on the spot.' Akilah ushers Lexy from her office and shuts the door, then flicks the catch and locks it. She sits down at her desk, '*Sex Sells*, bit of a clichéd name, sounds more like a farce than a drama.' Akilah splays her laptop and it springs into action, she scans the identity documents and photos using a small scanner next to the laptop; the screen displays *Earth Information Systems*.

MIX TO: Lexy, aka Kellyn Bell, wearing fish-net fingerless gloves, signs on the dotted line. She gives the assistant bank manager her most alluring look, drops the pen into her bag and waltzes out of the bank, trying not to finger the wads of notes. She stands in Piccadilly Gardens watching the fountain spurt and flurry, feeling a trickle of sweat run down her ear from under her wig.

CUT TO: There is a woman bouncer strutting on the steps in the orange city light as Lexy approaches, she nods in her direction and gestures with a sway of her arm for Lexy to enter. She teeters down the steps screwing her nose up at the sticky-and-stains smell wafting up. The walls of the club are castle-like; stripped stone with a rack of candles dripping red wax and black velvet drapes adorning the seating booths. The bar is fake oak and curves around the corner. Lexy glances around the room as she approaches the bar, catching a couple of gazes on the way; one from a woman in a faery-goth outfit and another from a cyber-punk. 'Which one?' she peruses as she waits for either to come and buy her a drink. The cyber-punk wins the lady! X, as she appears to want to be known, hands Lexy a glass of Kir-Royale and then escorts her to one of the booths. X is sporting a glass of green liquid and Lexy tries to guess its contents while she waits for X to begin the dance of seduction or deception, either will do. Lexy introduces herself as Jez much to X's delight and the game begins.

CUT TO: Interior, narrowboat, Kellyn is fucked by first a faery-goth and then a cyber-punk. Finally she says, 'bread' and the one named X brings her a glass of water. The sub-mission of the play is about to be revealed.

MIX TO: Interior, dressing room, Theatre on the

Canal, there's a knock at the door and it opens revealing Akilah holding a large bunch of pink lilies. Akilah kisses Lexy on her outstretched hand and then they raise their glasses. 'Here's to *Sex Sells*, it's gonna be one hell of a show.'

Kellyn is delivered back to Cassie's three days later. She's exhausted and ecstatic and sips on champagne as she waits for the woman at the bar to switch on the videotape, which has been returned with her.

FADE UP FROM BLACK: Lexy, as Jezebel, aka Jez E Bell enters the auditorium from the rear, the audience are watching the stage expectantly. Some have dressed for the occasion in top hat and tails, latex and rubber, and some have that lesbian couldn't-be-bothered-to-have-a-bath look. Jezebel swans down the aisle in an ivory pseudo-bodice, scant panties and crimson suspenders; she's mastered the art of her scarlet stilettos. Heads turn, hands applaud and she's flying towards the stage. Jezebel mounts the stage by pulling herself up with a rope suspended from the ceiling. She grabs a metal-grinder hanging from another rope and cranks it up. X enters by abseiling down and lands at Jezebel's feet; she's wearing a chained bra and a metal chastity belt, Jezebel aims the metal-grinder at it, the circular blade hits the belt and sparks fly, some into the audience who duck behind the row of seats in front. The women laugh, X remains still while Jezebel attacks the belt again, there is a shower of sparks which flutter through the air and land over the stage. X stands with her hands on her hips and stares at Jez as if waiting for an instruction.

'Welcome to the world of the three Xs, welcome to my world. One2one pages, you can bi, you can try, welcome one and all. Power tools and tampons, Pepsi and Nike, I'll force you to look, and next time you go for a six-pack I'll be your branded sex-pack. You're no perverted purchaser of porn, a humble consumer operating erotic deals from your remote-controlled sofa.' Lexy ties the metal-grinder back on the rope and it disappears above their heads.

Kellyn continues to watch the video, first smiling at Jez's portrayal of herself and then looking in disbelief as the play unfolds.

Mix to Scene 2: an advert for a retail adventure, fast-forward to Scene 5: Kellyn's voice on a Dick-tap-phone, fast-forward to Scene 7.

FADE UP: Jezebel, aka Jez E Bell, wearing Kellyn's Armani suit enters downstage, she fixes her gaze on the *Chairman Deluxe Office Massage Chair* centre stage; as she approaches she runs her hand along the top, somewhere between caressing it and dismissing it. 'Order, order, order and *I* have to submit, the order. Sell, sell and sell, self. Unique Selling Proposition, or is it Point? The point is to make money, or is it to make yourself?' Jezebel sits in the chair, picks up a copy of *Blue Ocean Strategy* and thumbs through it. 'Network and then market. The trick is to deceive, capture, steal, consume, consent and fantasise about what you'd do with the money.'

Kellyn orders a double JD on the rocks and gulps it down, she fast-forwards to the end of the tape and watches.

FADE TO: X kisses Jezebel, hard and hot on the lips, no fake acting-it kiss, they separate and X marches off stage to linger in the wings expectantly. Lexy takes centre stage, scanning the auditorium, scrutinising the standing audience clapping with the fervour of seals. She takes a deep bow, holds herself bent allowing the blood to rush to her head, savouring the dizzy glow of success.

MIX TO: Interior, passport control, two guards sporting machine guns watch the lines of passengers. Kellyn Bell, aka Lexy, wearing a cerise dress and bolero jacket lays her passport on the desk.

'Thank you, Ms Bell. Welcome to Mexico.'

CUT TO: Lexy digs her toes into the sand of the *playa* of Torre de Oro and slurps a large mouthful of champagne, she holds up the glass and admires the azure ocean sparkling behind the rising bubbles.

# MISHA HERWIN
## A Fairy's Story

I was born to be a good fairy. It was my destiny, or so my parents kept telling me. Poor old Plantain and Marigold, they did their best, but however hard they tried, it just didn't work. Learning spells did my head in, helping lame hedgehogs across the road and singing babies to sleep bored me stupid.

The real fun in life, I soon realised, lay in being bad. Bad fairies have a great time. If you don't believe me, read the stories. Who gets to do the prophesies, the glimpses into the future, that ruin everybody's lives? Who gets all the really revolting spells, the ones with lizard's gizzards and owl's bowels? Who rides on the backs of dragons and whips up storms? It's not us flower fairies, that's for sure.

Then there are the curses. I really go for curses. For a start, they can last for centuries and they've got this great habit of getting worse and worse as time goes on. They don't take much effort either. All you have to do is tell some trusting human that, from now on, they will be dogged by tragedy and misfortune and they are. Under the ladder they walk and down comes the concrete block. There's no will, no life insurance. They were too busy worrying about the fatal curse to sort it out. The ex-wife gets the lot, the kids starve and there's buckets and buckets of bad luck for everyone. Great!

The equipment's good too. No wanky wands, but needles and spindles and really sharp knives. The very thought made my fingers tingle in anticipation.

I threw away the petal skirt, cut my hair and started on my new life. I was full size by now. We good/bad fairies are human size. If we were only six inches high, the moment we turned up where we weren't wanted, someone would bring out the fly spray. The wings had dropped off too. They do after a bit. It's something to do with growing up.

First thing I did was change my name. Ditched the Rose part and became Bud. Got the gear. Jeans, a big leather belt, studs in the nose, the ears, the nipples and of course the belly button. Next came the boots. Saw them in the window, big and black with steel toe-caps, just right for kicking kittens. I knew I had to have them. I waited until the shop shut then I slid in through the keyhole and took them. It was my first bad deed and it felt great.

Mum and Dad were desperate. They tried being understanding, wanted me to see a counsellor, said it was a phase I was going through. Then, when things didn't get any better, they tried a few spells. I woke up one day with a mouth full of cobwebs. Couldn't speak for a week, but that didn't stop me. While I was waiting for the magic to wear off, I sat and perfected my glower. It got so good they couldn't stand to be in the same room. But whatever I did, they wouldn't throw me out. In the end I had no choice. I had to go.

I left, without saying goodbye, and made my way to the city. I was coming out of the station, when I saw him. Tall and blond, with broad shoulders and a bum you could die for. He was . . . well he was something else. Human unfortunately. It's a taboo. Cross-species copulation, the final barrier, the worst thing you can do. So, I went for it.

He'd just come out of the newsagent's and was standing there on the pavement zipping up his leather jacket. His helmet was slung over his arm, his bike was waiting at the kerb. Sleek and black with orange flames licking the shining metal. He was a dispatch rider, working for the hospital, racing against time to bring hearts and lungs and eyes to those who waited so desperately for a transplant.

An angel of mercy and me a bad fairy. It gave me the shivers and it wasn't just to do with being bad. There was a warm quivery feeling, like the furry softness on the underside of a moth's wing, fluttering around inside me. I parked my gum in the corner of my mouth and walked over.

'Hi,' I said, 'great bike.'

He looked at me and his eyes were as blue as a summer sky.

'It's a Fireblade,' he said, his hand stroking the curve of the tank.

The ground flipped under my feet. I couldn't catch my breath. I knew I wasn't his type, but it didn't matter. That's where magic comes in. I fixed him with my green eyes and he was lost.

'Want a ride?' he said.

I climbed on behind him and wrapped my arms around his waist. I pressed my cheek against the warm leather of his jacket and breathed in his smell. He started the engine. The bike kicked into life, throbbing between my legs as we roared down the street. The wind tore through my hair. Lights whirled like a thousand exploding stars. I never wanted it to end.

Then we went back to his place and did what humans do. It wasn't bad. Almost as good as the bike.

I changed my style. I went a bit soft. I wore long black dresses and painted my lips and nails scarlet. He called me his little witch and we were good together. For a while.

The trouble with humans is their bodies. They can't leave them alone. They have to keep filling them with food and drink. A sip of nectar keeps me going for weeks. I never need to go to supermarkets. I never shop. And that was the problem. He couldn't understand why there was never any food in the house. An empty fridge, that was what finished us.

He came in from work one night and I could see he was tired. His face was pinched and pale.

'Come and sit down and let me run my fingers through your hair,' I murmured.

'I'm starving,' he said. 'What's for tea?'

Whoops! I clapped my hand over my mouth. I'd forgotten. I hadn't been near a supermarket for days.

'Kiss me,' I whispered seductively.

'I'm hungry,' he snarled, his jaw tense.

'I know,' I soothed.

'Then why the hell don't you do something about it?'

'I'm sorry,' I shrugged. 'I was . . .'

'You were sitting on your butt.'

'It's a very pretty butt,' I put on a little girl voice and fluttered my lashes.

It didn't work. I thought he was going to hit me. I shrank back against the wall as he charged towards me.

'Pizza,' he growled, grabbing the phone. My mouth watered. I think I was becoming used to human food.

'Make mine a margherita,' I said.

He glared at me as if I was slug slime and stamped off to the bathroom. I couldn't help it. Honestly I couldn't. I was so angry. How dare he speak to me like that? Treating me as if I was some little tart, as if I hadn't broken all the rules just to be with him. I raised my hand and the power zapped out of my fingers, before I could stop it.

It zoomed across the room, bounced off the walls and slammed him right between the shoulder blades.

There was a sizzle and a strange watery smell. The air wobbled and I fell back on the sofa. My head was spinning and my arms and legs felt heavy and weak. I lay there completely wiped out, until the door bell rang and someone shouted through the letter box, 'Pizza.'

I'd forgotten all about it, but after using all that energy I thought, why not?

'Come on in, it's open,' I said.

He nudged the door with his elbow and stepped inside. He was carrying two boxes, balancing one on top of the other and he couldn't see where he was going. Something crunched beneath his foot. It wasn't his fault.

He rubbed his shoe on the carpet, leaving a smear of blood and guts behind him. I picked up the poor little frog and held it in the palm of my hand. It was quite flat. Its entrails were on the sole of the delivery boy's shoe.

I stroked its smooth green skin, I whispered in its ear and I wondered what would happen if I gave it a kiss . . .

Then I took it by the leg and flushed it down the toilet.

# JO STANLEY
## Die, You Bastard

Cancer! Kann sirrr! It ate me without me spying it. First the bastard invaded my lungs, then it rampaged into my liver, spreading secondaries there. The sneaky git captured and devoured me while I was getting on with life as a woman who lived to walk wild spaces. It stole up on the me who was too focused on doing any old job that would feed my roaming habit. I used to go away for months at a time, walking long-distance paths in the Appalachians and South America. And the job that best permitted this expensive habit had been as residential social worker supporting young people with learning difficulties in shared houses. It paid well, if you did sleep-overs. And there was always a demand for relief workers, espccially those who'd do weekends. So I could pick work up again easily each time I came back from a trek.

So, focused on earning for the next trip, I neglected my body's hints. And late-diagnosed cancer is the reason I find myself sitting in a public sitting room whose pinkness makes me want to scream, on top of everything else that makes me want to scream. I put 'kind' people at the top of my list. God spare me from the conciliatory, from soft-voiced ladies who don't look you in the eye, who skirt that word that begins with 'd' and ends with 'th' and prefer to say 'no longer with us'. If there's one thing I can't stand it's denial. And even in hospices, that ultimate place of facing the truth, there is frighteningly little deep tackling. There were no stamping maniacs ranting, 'Why me,' and 'Fuck this' and 'Why can't you bloody well cure me, you incompetent cunts?' Not till me, that is. The nurses had me written down as 'a difficult patient', who was 'having trouble coming to terms with her diagnosis'. I know that because I demanded to see my records. Which is not what dying people are supposed to do. But meek acceptance of bureaucratic rules never has been my number. And stroppiness seems a perfectly fair response to having your life chopped short. Call it staff training: to encounter this raging bull-roaring lion in a too-tight cage. They should charge me for raising their awareness of responses to terminal diagnosis.

It's Tuesday, two pm I've just finished my post-lunch rampage and am resting before my pre-tea, upset-everyone-you-can session. You come in, Kat, accompanied by Rukshana, an associate nurse who fades back towards the ward office rather than risk another tirade.

You, my old walking partner. You enter with a bunch of freesias, not a compass, in your hands. Now you wear a chic leather jacket the colour of midnight, not some sturdy waterproof made by North Face. Your trousers have creases in the right places; they're not your usual crumpled, pilled jogging bottoms. Instead of a sleeping-bag-stuffed rucksack you have an Elvis shoulder bag, and your face has no protective grease, your head no micropore cap.

You hesitate at the edge of the lounge. Hospices try hard but they never make their lounges like ordinary living rooms. There is never any evidence of slobbery about: no discarded beer cans or empty pizza boxes or a scrawled-on *Radio Times*. No tights hanging drying on a radiator rack. No sounds of rowing neighbours through the walls. Here I am on show, a neatly washed and dressed product of their ministrations, as is the room.

I guess you aren't sure it's me, over here by the

window. I look a sight, almost unrecognisable. The steroids have swelled me into Mrs Blobby. The chemotherapy stole my lovely brown hair, and now I look like a coconut part-barbered by someone who became absent-minded with the thinning scissors. My face is so pallid that if I were a suet pudding they'd have to put colouring in to make me marketable. In fact, I doubt I'd be allowed on the shop shelf.

'Hi, Trish.' Your voice is a bit hesitant; you look from slightly under your eyebrows.

'Wotcha.' I'm gruff.

'Sorry I didn't manage to get to see you before.'

I've been in only five days. 'Well, there's not much point in seeing me anyhow!' I grouch. I am surprised how much hostility I feel even to her. Where's my affection gone? I sound like a wrestler rejecting an opponent's overtures after losing a bout. 'I look like shite – so no one in their right mind would *want* to see me. And I haven't got a fucking thing of interest to say, and I'm too bloody narky to be a listener. So I guess I'm best left to stew in my own juice . . . And it's a bitter juice, actually, so steer clear of the stink.'

I stare at the huge TV with its attendant videos: the whole *Carry On* series; *Dances with Wolves*; *The Two Ronnies*. I glare at the neat row of donated *Reader's Digest* condensed books in leather-look bindings and the shelf of spoken word cassettes: Kate Adie's autobiography; *Sense and Sensibility*; *The Best of The Navy Lark*. How meaningless everything is. And yet how poignantly meaningful. What can I care about any more? Why should anything interest me? I won't let it.

'Trish, I'm so sorry this has happened to you.'

'Then try multiplying it tenfold to see how I feel!' As I slam my fist into the chair arm, I'm shocked to realise I am enjoying being so horrible. This is a treat.

It's the first chance I've had since the diagnosis to be truly narky with anyone other than medics. And I want to go on being absolutely filthy, a real bitch of the first order. Ungrateful, unfair, incompliant and absolutely unladylike. Who can I start on next? Yes, family. Every visitor. The hospice chaplain. Whoopee, I've got nearly a score of potential victims.

'Is there anything I can do for you?' You sit down on the right end of the sofa, by the *Hello!*s and the *Good Housekeeping*s. Why the hell can't there be piles of *Back Street Heroes* and *Divas*, *New Scientist*s and *Wired*s? Why does a vacuous atmosphere have to accompany palliative care? I'd like to throw the pots of fake pot-pourri through the glass of every 'suitable' picture on the wall: the framed twee poems with discrete flowers decorating their edges, the preachy messages in their peachy mounts. I want broken glass here, blood, chaos and real life – anything that breaks beyond the bounds of wall-to-wall Niceness. As never before I understand the young men who used to be my clients: the pleasure and temporary power of delinquency as a riposte to other people's restrictions.

I kick my wheelchair step as hard as my bedraggled once-legs can manage. The metal looks like a bit of new fire escape, but I'll do no more running downstairs again. If there are fires I'll fry. I won't be able to rescue people.

'Not a fucking thing. Not you, not anyone.'

You watch me. And I look out of the window at the sky so purply-black with storm clouds. We've walked moors and mountains in weather like this, stripped off in rainstorms and danced in high places. We've loved extremes. And now you'll go there with someone else, never me again.

There's a question most people don't dare to ask.

It's 'how long?' I wonder if you'll inquire. You always want to know parameters and probabilities. How long a walk will be. How low the temperature. What's the severest altitude someone could survive in without oxygen. What is the incidence of grizzly bears attacking hikers in these woods. How likely is the snow at this time of year.

Instead you say, 'We could go to the edge of the moors, sit in one of those pubs where we used to go after walks. Somewhere in Edale perhaps, wherever you fancy.'

'How?'

'I can borrow a Motability car from work. And the sister said you can go out in the wheelchair.'

'I can do anything I bloody want,' I protest, affronted at the idea that anyone can control my mobility. It's preposterous – and horribly possible. I could be trapped in pinkness forever.

You look at me, Kat, and I know you want to cry. I do too, but I won't let myself.

'You know what I want? To paint their whole place scarlet and black. To kick ten-gallon paint cans over and then ride over them in my wheelchair until I turn the whole hospice into a bad Jackson Pollock painting: just mess and outrage. And then scream and scream. There is too much silence in this place, too much restraint on noisy feeling. Too much avoidance of nasty truths, like DEATII, DEATH, DEATH!'

You regard me with your steady eyes and repeat. 'To the moors.'

I jerk my brake off and yank my wheelchair away from you, careering round the room, scuffing and ramming the hapless sofas as if I was on the dodgems. You've put freedom and a refusal of boundaries in my mind. I'm suddenly thinking of the mass trespass on Kinder Scout in nineteen thirty-two.

Five hundred Manchester ramblers and a score from Sheffield asserted that all human beings have a right to walk their land. The landowner claimed it was private land. But posterity knows they demonstrated, they asserted a precedent about rights to roam that still endures.

But this is two thousand and six and I want to somehow insist – as if I was a crowd and not a singular unit – on my own right to freely roam the wild lands of anger. I want to say this earth is big and full of many kinds of places. And it is my right to walk – or wheelchair over – them all. No one can tell me that death and dying should be a quiescent business, a tucked-away business. It's my right to roam through the whole spectrum of emotions. Nobody is the landowner of the dying process. No one can bar any path to any terrain of feeling.

'Yes,' I sigh, and add loudly, 'I'd bloody love to.'

You grin and grip my hand, as we so often did to help each other up steep rock faces.

'Atta girl!'

*

The days have passed and I've been driven mad, as I have for the last month, by the kind of support that goes with death. I have sat in the big, height-adjustable bed with its green waterproof mattress cover and rose-pink counterpane and suffered hour after hour of misery in my body. I have endured cartloads of tentative inquiries by people who can do nothing for me, so should stay out of the way. A million acts of irritating kindness. Two million solicitous questions. Twenty million glances laden with pity like chandeliers are burdened with candles.

They want to know why I didn't know that my

cough was lung cancer, why I didn't go to the doctor earlier and whether I regret working with all the chain-smokers whose cigarettes were probably the cause of my destruction. Don't I want to try some alternative treatment, like at Bristol? No, I don't want to drive myself nuts seeking impossible cures when I've only got about three weeks left to live. It's too bloody late to tolerate still more people poking at my body.

They come bearing irrelevant objects 'that I might need' from my flat in Didsbury, or presents that are so inappropriate that I realise the buyers must have been casting around with manic desperation. Tokens offered in place of words that can't be found. Less and less they know what to say to me, now that death is so near that it becomes even more unimaginable to those whose ends look far away.

I survive the soggy onslaught, not quite engulfed by the tyrannous slagheap of concern, concern and concern. And I long for frankness, for air of every kind.

I've looked forward to this outing to Edale with you. The drive from Manchester takes maybe fifty minutes. I drink a margarita, you a Perrier, at the Swan with Two Necks. We sit in the conservatory, whose windows look out over a sweep of moorland. The barman places our glasses on mats made from old hunting prints. Peacefully, I notice that no saboteur has stuck anti-hunt slogans over the red-coated chaps and their flotillas of hounds. And I find it oddly easy to be nice to you, though your painstaking politeness is almost unbearable. Oh, for a rough, 'come on, slow coach', like it used to be.

After twenty minutes, when I've recovered from the journey from car to bar, I suddenly feel impatient and wheel myself over to the pub's French windows. You open the doors for me, and sweep them clear of the mock-tapestry curtains that brush the green carpet. And I find myself wheeling out onto the lawn, and then down the York stone path to the boundary wall, then the edge of the moors. Oh God, to get some lungfuls of wild air at least; to see space and stark colours. I wheel back to fetch you.

'Come on, Kat, let's go out in all this,' I yell at you still lounging by the log-effect gas fire in the Tudor hearth.

You ease out to join me. 'I'm not sure how far I can push you in a wheelchair on this terrain.' You stand there assessing the wetness of the soil, the rake of the slope, the number and height of tussocks and your own posh town boots. And you smile, 'Let's try' and pile on my layers of outerwear again.

We manage to get a surprisingly long way, quite near to a place where there is a drop into a deep valley. The further we proceed, and the more I breathe in this fresh free air, the more I realise what I want to do.

It's not that I want to admire the view. It's that I long to melt into it, become just another hillock in the landscape: my bones on this earth, and my remains fertilising the land.

Pity I couldn't have dressed better for the part. Such an occasion would merit a robe of peat, a ceremonial gown fit to greet the soil. Instead my swollen spare tyres are shoehorned into a bundle of outsize interlock that smells of hospice detergent and reeks of my now-manky body. I am a swaddled, mountainous wreck. Sorry about the disrespect, earth, I apologise as I survey this beautiful space that I long to be my home. I didn't know I was coming – for this.

'Push me over it, Kat. Give me a good shove,' I find myself pleading. 'That's what I want. An end.

Here.'

'Oh, darling, I can't do that. And I think you know I can't.'

'Yes, you bloody can,' I eyeball you, like a ringmaster. 'Just tell them it was an accident. My wheelchair lost control. You couldn't yank it back. Tragic. Misadventure. And it'll save several weeks' money that would otherwise be pointlessly spent on my palliative bloody care.'

'I couldn't even watch you die. I certainly couldn't kill you, Trish. Be fair. You're asking too much, darling. I can't.'

My lip curls. 'I hate you, you bastard. Do what I bloody well say!' And I wheel round so that my back is to you. 'Sod off. Go. You're no use to me. Call yourself a friend. Stuff you.'

It's very quiet here, just the sound of some distant birds newly returned from wherever they wintered. January is too early for spring lambs. The cars on the Stockport road are so far away that we can barely hear them. I marshal my venom. I plan to beat you.

'So you'd let your wimpy scruples get in the way of my best interests?' I demand.

You look at me for a long time. Then you swallow.

'Ermmm . . . yes, it seems that I would. Appallingly cowardly, isn't it,' you acknowledge quietly. 'I'm sorry.'

You are pulling your blue mittens on and off, on and off, in anxiety, like an obsessive hand-washer. You huddle your chin down into your fleece, breathing into its unzipped collar, gazing everywhere assessingly, reflectively. Avoiding my eyes.

'I *am* disgusted with you,' I glare, pulling your attention back to me. Get on with it, girl! I want to yell.

'Actually, I feel disgusted with myself, as well as right.' Your voice has *gravitas*, and I can see you trembling.

I look at you for a long time. You look back. Then you look away again. Are you disgusted by my cantankerous demands? This much should not be asked of a friendship. What a bully I've become, I think. What a git. But I'm going to get my way.

I've never seen you cry, in all the fifteen years we've been walking together. But as I ease round to the side of you, I see your wobbling lips. I'm not sure if it's love for me that's upsetting you so, or despair at your own lack of bravery that you are suddenly confronting. Or fear of being prosecuted for aiding and abetting a death, even murder, for who is to prove that I asked for this?

'Kill me, you bastard,' I insist.

'I can't, Trish. I can't.'

'You could, if you cared enough.'

'It's not like that, Trish,' you shake your head. 'It's not,' you add quietly, almost to yourself.

'For God's sake, give me the finish I deserve. Shove me hard, now!' I insist again, voice like hot vinegar, rasping your soft doubts like a metal grater.

You walk for ten paces or so, circle round and round, round and round. Then you come back to me. Your poor suede boots with their clever hand-stitching are now wrecked. You'll never wear them to Cornerhouse movies or galleries in Princess Street again.

'I'll try,' you murmur, finally. 'If that's what you really want.'

The sigh that comes out of me is enough to power a windmill for a week. 'I do.'

'And if you think your family will be able to cope with this kind of end. I mean, people usually want a last few weeks of slowly saying goodbye, Trish.'

'I don't know,' I hesitate. 'I don't know what they can handle, at all. But I know what *I* want. So, please . . .'

We look around. There is no one here, it's too early in the season for most people. And, being a weekday, there are no hardy climbers or walkers around. We are not overlooked. It's possible.

You walk the bank, assessing where the slope is steepest, where the bottom is most rocky.

'You'll probably get badly bruised before you break your neck,' you advise.

'I know. But I'll try and somersault myself forward so that I go quick and hard. That should work. Use my body-weight, God knows there's enough of it now.'

There is something about talking so sensibly about my movements, like planning where to picnic, that is somehow unbearable.

'I can't,' you plead again, and start crying. And I can see that I could probably not kill me, either, if I was in your shoes. Especially at such short notice. I wonder if I can provoke a row with you, and make you so angry that you want to fling me over. Then I realise that that is unfair. I should be responsible for my own death.

I relent. 'Look, Kat, go back to the pub. Pretend you've left your scarf there, and just let me do it on my own, I can probably manage.' It seems only fair.

'But you can only manage about eight turns of the wheel, on this terrain,' you protest. 'So you can't get far enough by yourself. I've seen how quickly your arms get tired. Anyway, I couldn't let you die on your own . . . I couldn't.'

'It might be easier for me,' I lie.

You shake your head. 'Oh God, shall I be that

bastard then? Shall I really push my favourite friend down a mountain?' you ask yourself, pacing dementedly. I pity you. Maybe I should just turn away and go, and put up with death in the hospice instead. But I am mean to you one more time, because I feel horrified at the thought of expiring in that pink place, in Niceness-opolis.

'Yes, be that bastard,' I tell you, trying to compel you with my eyes.

And then you really cry. Your whole body shakes. Your shoulders twitch and shudder as if an electric current was ricocheting its way through you.

Still I wait and watch. I will you to help me go. Oh, it takes you a long, long time to stop sobbing.

Finally you look down at me, red-eyed. I stick my lower lip out obdurately. You want a farewell conversation with me, don't you, about all the years of our friendship and what I've meant to you, etc. Well, I don't. I can't afford such tenderness. I just want to be a bag of bones at the bottom of the valley, decomposing in organic harmony with the old vegetation and vestiges of fallen sheep.

You lightly kiss the back of my shoulder, so briefly. You know I'll crumple if there is any softness going on.

And finally you manage the terminal shove, taking a run and using all your body to slam me forward. The jolt propels the wheelchair nearly ten feet. I start to roll. It's not fast, for all that you've rammed into me as fiercely as you can. For a moment I'm reminded of Mum, refusing to push me dangerously high on the swings in Crowcroft Park when I was little. I always did like danger, so here's the final thrill, at last. You've acceded. Bless you. If only the roll was faster, the hill steeper.

'This is the most unbastardly thing you've ever

done,' I call. My voice judders as the bumpy ground disrupts me. Can you even make out what I'm saying, from back there? Are you crying so hard that you can't see? However will you cope with the drive back, and the reporting of this to the hospice? How can I help it be okay for you?  I can't.

One of my poxy shawls flies off, then a loose scarf, the one you bought me in Kendal. I throw off my over-gloves, then my under-gloves, then the rug over my knees. If only I'd thought to ditch my coat. Let hypothermia get me if the tumble doesn't.

I'd like to call back, 'thank you, love'. But I'm already too far gone for you to hear me. Anyway, I can't afford to turn round. I need to face my end so that I can do it efficiently. Finally, the pace increases. It's a bit like being in a dodgem car that's got loose, a swing that has done what grown-ups always warn swings will do: fly off and kill you. I'm only terrified that the ruts will bump me out of the chair, or overturn me, before I can get to the more drastic drop that'll kill me properly.

But then I lurch off over the edge, and hurl myself as much as I can. I go down, down. I'm taking possession of the land my way. I'm joining it in all its muddy, fertile unpinkness.

# BRIGHID ROSE
## Wallpapering

My other lovers had either left, died or gone mad. That's how it seemed. I was looking for a cheap thrill. Something comforting. A warm body in a cold bed. Something to stave off those dark, lonely nights.

He seemed the perfect choice: family man, father of three, semi-committed spouse. I thought I could have a night of excitement and that would be it, he'd go back to the life he'd come from. But no.

I thought he said his name was Liam. It was noisy in the place where I met him. It turned out his name was Ian. I'd kicked off with the usual; eye-contact, prolonged eye-contact, edging closer along the bar, leaving him to make the first move so he feels like a man, etc. Eventually he comes over, offers to buy me a drink. I say 'yes', so he knows he's in with a shout. Then he compliments me, tells me I look nice (I've only dressed for the sex; a get-up that yells, 'Fuckmedaddyoh'.) I act flattered, 'how kind of you to say so.' Make him feel like a hero, like he's God's gift to women and it goes on from there, blah, blah, blah, until the end of the night, when he whispers, 'I want to make love to you.' And I'm so coy he thinks it's been his idea all along; that the thought's never entered my head. The upshot of all this is he's home late and has to explain to his wife. Whereas me, I don't have to explain to anyone.

I thought I'd leave it at that. I thought he would too. But that wasn't the end of the story. Not by a long chalk. I bump into him again, a different bar this time, but the same scenario. I give him the usual chatter. *Oh, really? I never realised that cricket/*

*computers/weight training/diesel engines could be so interesting* . . . And then, at the end of the night, when everything's done and dusted and it's time to leave, instead of just upping off back to his lovely life, he asks for my phone number.

People have made comments, they've told me I'm the self-destructive type. But that's not the half of it. What I like is to bring everyone else down with me. I like things tipping over the edge. I like to see the whole tea-set, the cups, saucers, plates, jugs, pots, knives, forks, spoons crashing off the end of the table onto the floor. Doesn't matter if I'm underneath, it all coming down on top of me. I'm too enamoured by the noise. I like it too much when things break.

I'd like to be able to say there was a valid reason for what I did; for example, because I loved the man; because he made me feel good; because it was the best sex; or because I was, at the least, a little obsessed. But none of that's the case. Somewhere in my head, I must have twigged that Ian, whatever his name was, was a chance to see plates fall, to hear some loud noise. However much you tell yourself that *this time* you're after a gentler ride, still another part of you is all out for trouble. There's just something about putting yourself in the eye of a storm, being the *cause* of it.

He rings up and asks me out to dinner. I think about it for a moment and then say, 'all right then', because I hardly ever eat out so there'd be novelty value to it at least. Hand on heart, at that point I hadn't anything else in mind. Just dinner and sex. Nothing more than that.

He takes me to a low-lit place over on the opposite side of town from where he lives. When we get there, he wants to tell me his life story. In depth. I learn the details of his working day as regional manager for a chain that sells electronic equipment. I hear about the current value of his house and how long he's lived in it. I hear about the kids; what they're all called and about their different character traits. He practically gives me a school report for each offspring. Then he tells me about Annette, who's wonderful it seems but who's also a little busy right now/is rather engaged with work/is difficult to understand sometimes/has a tendency to be remote/has no sex-drive. He confides how many times he's cheated on her; only three lovers in fourteen years he says (not including me). I know the next bit's coming then. He starts to try and justify it to himself; why it's okay for him to be there with me, about to put a hand on my thigh and go up my skirt. I sit listening. It all sounds so rational and reasonable. At least the words do if you separate them out. As for their overall meaning, they don't make any sense at all. It's such a convoluted, twisted, fucked-up argument that I lose track of what he's saying. I sit thinking, *gibberishgobbledygookmumbo jumbo.* It's plain old adultery after all. No use in trying to dress it up as something else.

He makes his life sound fantastic. He says he likes to see to it that things follow sound rules. He says that most of his life-criteria have been fulfilled already. He's just about ticked all his boxes, he says. He even thinks I can be fitted neatly into the general scheme of things and that's what really gets to me.

I watch his clean fingers twirling the stem of his wine glass around and he keeps on with it, telling me his philosophies on life. But a familiar feeling has started up in me. I can feel myself toughening as he talks, hardening from the inside, railing in my head. I'm getting angry in that *cold* way. People describe anger as a hotness, something that makes them act rashly. It doesn't get me like that. Mine's cold and slow; water turning to ice. I know what's doing it this time, it's his talk about families. I sit resisting it. I never did feel easy with the whole family thing.

As a diversion, I start to imagine his house, the family home. I imagine the wallpaper; tasteful, decorative, following a repeated design into every corner. The same pattern, over and over. It's not such a strong fantasy at first, but I imagine marks being put on it; a sort of blotching that upsets the overall design. I start imagining the house next door, the family that lives there. In my head, their home has exactly the same wallpaper. The same colour and everything. Then I imagine all the houses, all the families living on that road, all the houses on that side of town, the paper on every one of those walls following the same pattern. The smudges start coming thick and fast until whole streets' worth of wallpaper are ruined by the marks. There I go, full-pelt with one of my fantasies, getting all amused just thinking about it. But then the waiter comes over to the table with a dessert menu and that ends my little train of thought and, for a while, Ian's lecture on life.

After the meal, we go to a hotel. He pays for the room, just as he has for the meal. He'll be earning about four times as much as I am, I figure, so I'm not going to get shame-faced about it. We go up to the room and before long I'm taking off my clothes and so is he. I like to see him naked. Not so much because his body turns me on. It's an average enough body, I don't dislike it. But it's his nakedness that I like; the big-man suit removed to show his white skin. It makes him look so *susceptible* and that's what does it for me. I bite him so that I can see my imprint in his skin, and he seems to like it too.

When it's time for him to leave, and he's sitting on the bed tying up his laces, he turns to me and says straight up, without a hint of mockery in his voice, 'I *like* you. You're a keeper.' I smile my most gracious smile and wonder what in Heaven's name he's going to say next.

'How about another evening next week, babe?' He actually calls me *babe* and I don't even bat an eyelid. It's obvious after three nights together that there's a certain momentum to all this. I think, *what the hell?* I decide to just go along with it and agree to meet him the following Thursday. He goes home, and I fall asleep in the king-sized hotel bed.

Around this point, after the meal, is probably where the trouble-hungry part kicks off and starts sniffing for the possibility of a big kind of ruckus, although to be fair, I'm not *planning* anything yet. I fall asleep after the sex and it would seem that all the anger from the restaurant has gone away. I'm as meek as a lamb. But then, that night I dream I'm in a forest with a can of fluorescent paint going merrily about the trees spraying them with crosses, picking out which ones are dead wood.

*

I suppose somewhere along the line I must have got fed-up. I must've sensed that my only hold over anyone was going to be the bodily sort; a worse-than-useless, tits-and-arse kind of power. I'm not blessed with marvellous brains. I wasn't born into heaps of money. The only clout a girl like me was going to have was the power to turn a few heads, to make eyes bulge, to make a few dicks go stiff. Most types of bloke – they're pretty instinctual creatures, all told.

Only problem with that though is it doesn't last.

At some stage it's going to dawn on you that your youth isn't going to last forever, and that's when some deep-down part of you thinks, *fuck it*, and you start trying to milk it for all it's worth. While you still can. You set about fuelling yourself up before your skin starts sagging from your bones, before your teeth start rotting in your head and all the paltry power you had is gone.

It's not all bad though. There are tricks to be learnt along the way to help you. Tricks you learn in childhood and build upon as an adult. Tricks that enabled you to eke something nearing affection out of your charmingly fuck-witted parents when you were knee-high, and that, later, you come to use so naturally, so effortlessly on your lovers. You should see me in action. I'm a master magician.

Let me spell it out; just how those little tricks work when you know how to handle yourself. First there's the rudimentaries that everyone's familiar with: the slap going on your cheeks, your eyes, your lips and the right get-up going on over your curves, highlighting your advantages, covering up your drawbacks. Then you're out there at the hot spots and sooner or later you start catching their eye. Using tits-and-arse power, you hopefully manage to keep a good hold over them and from there things start to get more sophisticated. You get them talking, all the while making yourself as blank as possible. You're the pretty, non descript face, the attentive listener, the personable person. They love that because in their heads they can turn you into whatever they like; the woman of their dreams. Meanwhile you're the regular devil in disguise.

The next step is to read them for clues. You're hanging back working out what they're into so you know what you're going to feed them: whether to be the sub or the dom; the chaste and virtuous maiden; the motherly care-taker; the aloof and enigmatic siren; the dark, vampish bloodsucker; or the sluttish prick tease.

When they start showing signs of real interest, you mirror them back a little, not too much, and slowly you get under their skin. They start to say predictable things like, 'I've never talked with anybody like this before,' or, 'You remind me so much of my first true love/my fantasy cartoon heroine/my favourite actress/my mother.' You're nothing of the sort, of course, but still, the illusion's there and so you're on to a winner. Things are going according to plan.

The final stage is when they start to *need* you. Once you've reached that point, you just have to keep stoking the fire, as it were, and then you can pretty much do what you want. It can feel quite heady, like you're on a kind of spree. The amazing thing is that for ages you might not even realise you're doing it. Any of it. You learnt the methods so early, and you're making use of them so seamlessly, that you're flying on automatic pilot. It's going well, you feel good, you don't question it. Until it stops working. And I'm not claiming that it works every time either, on every single bloke. There are exceptions. But I'd say the success rate is a good seven out of ten. And as long as you don't make the mistake of expecting to live happily ever after with whoever it is, it's fine. All you're wanting is to keep that lonely old wolf from the door.

Anyway, Ian. Poor Ian. Ages before I met him, I had the necessary skills honed. It was second nature to me. He came along and went in way over his head.

\*

The next thing that happens is he asks me to go away

with him for the weekend. See how it follows such a typical course? It's sweet when you think about it. It's so *routine.*

He tells his wife a new set of lies; bigger ones. Then we head off to a hotel in the country and maybe I'm not the first woman he's been there with because he knows his way around the place like it's the back of his hand.

He takes me for walks in the hotel grounds and into the surrounding countryside. He has a map of footpaths in the area and he's planned out the routes. He has a silver hip-flask with whiskey in it to sip on the way and you can tell it makes him feel upmarket by the way he drinks from it. I realise it's ages since I've been walking in the countryside with a bloke. (With the previous one it was all coming back from work to find him still in bed watching motor racing on the TV, the sound turned up so loud that next-door kept banging on the wall; my cue to start shouting.)

This time though, I'm lapping up the luxury in the presence of Mr Retail Outlet. I act my part well; all wide-eyed at his generosity, and then even Little-Miss-Hell-To-Live-With can seem like an okay date.

That weekend I bathe in the *en suite* bathroom, get a facial in the beauty rooms, drink the miniatures in the minibar, dress to go down for evening meals and even call my mother from the hotel-room bed. Then, on the Sunday we go for another walk and as I'm climbing over a style, he offers me his hand like he's an old-fashioned gent in a period drama, and doesn't let go of it once I'm down on the other side. He squeezes my fingers in an attempt to be affectionate and then wants to hold my hand as we carry on the walk. I'm not sure what to make of it. I don't feel comfortable. My arm goes stiff.

Then, in the car on the way back to town, he's quiet as a mouse. Not his usual self at all. None of his putting-the-world-to-rights talk. He drives his saloon car, staring ahead at the road and hardly says a word. When he pulls up outside my flat and I'm about to climb out of the passenger seat, he lets out a sob. I turn to look at him and he breaks down crying. I close the car door.

'What's the matter?'

He can't speak right away.

Eventually, he says how he can't bear to go home and how he hates his life and how his wife makes him feel unwanted and all about how unhappy he is. I sit and pat his arm.

'There, there . . .'

It takes him a while to calm down, to be all right enough to drive himself home. When he's more or less settled, I tell him that I'll see him soon, and I get out of the car. He drives off and I go up to my flat. I turn on the kettle and make myself a strong cup of tea. I can tell that something big is about to start. Trouble is about to kick off and I'm a bit high from the feeling of it. I sit down and ready myself.

I'm spot on. Things escalate from there. Within a week, he rings to say that he's had a row with his wife. She's accused him of having an affair. In retaliation, he's accused her of a whole load of things; being unsupportive, uncaring, etc, told her that he needs a break from her and wants to move out. He's even started looking for somewhere else to live.

The next day I'm at work and I can't stop thinking about it. I'm turning someone over on their mattress so they don't get bedsores, and a flush comes over me. I feel gratified, sort of pumped up. I think of the lengths he's going to when I've only known him for a little over three weeks. It's a confirmation of something in a way. Proof. But mostly it's the thrill, the sense of excitement, wondering what's going to happen next.

Within a few days he's found a house to rent. Luckily, it's even handier for work and the motorway junction, he says. He's trying to sound bright on the phone but you can tell he's acting braver than he feels. He asks me to come and visit him there. He says it'll help him to settle in. I go round and he's got a mark on his face where she's hit him. It's like I've landed a part in a film; a trashy, predictable one that's made for TV and that's what's fun about it.

There's hardly anything in the house. There's a sofa and a huge old television in the lounge, beds in the bedrooms and a cooker and fridge in the kitchen. That's it, apart from a couple of his suits and shirts slung over the arm of the sofa and a carton of milk and an oven-ready meal in the fridge.

I ask him how long he's staying there. He says that he's not going back to her, that he's done it because of me, that I made him realise something he was blind to before or some other rubbish. Then he orders a take-away from a place that delivers to the door, and we sit and eat it watching your average evening's programmes on that massive old telly, except I eat most of the food because he says he isn't hungry.

The next time I go round there, he's looking a bit worse for wear. He needs a shave and he has dark patches under his eyes. He seems on edge. I'm not there very long when he says he wants to call his kids. He goes into the next room to make the call but I can still hear him talking. It's his wife who answers and they have a big slanging match. Then she puts the kids on the line to speak to their abandoning father and it seems they're crying down the phone, not understanding what's happened to their loving family. I sit and follow the conversation via the one half of it I can hear; the desperately placating, pacifying tones he uses with his children. I imagine the frantic high-pitched twitter at the other end of the phone, the strange bewildered voices. I sit quietly as the chaos spins past.

Then things go up a gear. His wife says that she isn't going to let him see the kids. She gets the locks on the doors changed so that he can't get in, not even to get more clothes. She writes him a letter. In it she describes the consequences of his actions upon the family. She says that she's off work and on tranquillisers and that the kids are starting to have problems too. One of the kids has been wetting the bed, has nightmares, has been waking up crying in the night. Another won't talk, wanders around in a sullen, withdrawn state and the other, the eldest, is probably going to fail her exams. The man's only been gone a couple of weeks. Anyhow, he's not allowed to see the children and the grandparents are coming to live in the house to help calm them down. Apparently, his parents-in-law now consider him to be beneath contempt.

The threats, the accusations, the point-scoring; everybody's seen it. It's all happened before, numerous times, but it's still interesting to watch. And somehow, throughout it all, I'm feeling better and better; more settled, more calm. As though, as a result of all the mess, something has been balanced, sorted out, put right.

Ian threatens his wife with a solicitor's letter. She relents and allows him to see the children. He asks me if I'll come round to meet them when he brings them back to his house, but I say no. Anyone with sense would realise that was a bad idea but I suppose he isn't thinking straight. He goes back to the family home to pick the kids up and I imagine the visit; his wife refusing to come downstairs and see him, the children angry and sullen, slouched on the living room chairs, an atmosphere in the place like pure torture, and him amongst it all not having a clue what to say to any of them.

I can see it clearly; he's a changed man. Already, when I look at him, I can see that the wind has gone out of him. He's let the rented place get in a state. He hasn't taken the rubbish out. He sits indoors with his coat on and I half expect the buttons to be done up wrong. When I ask him a question, it takes him ages to answer; his head's too full of other things that he's raking over. He says that none of it means anything without me there, although I'm pretty sure he still doesn't have a clue who I am. It doesn't stop him asking me to move in with him though.

I tell him, *Thanks, but no thanks. I like things as they are.*

He isn't happy about it, mind.

He says, *I did this for you . . . I thought it's what you wanted . . . You owe it to me to give me support.*

To keep him quiet I say, *okay then, we'll see.* Although I know perfectly well that we won't.

He starts to take some time off work. Mr High-Achiever is showing signs of slackening. It's just a few days here and there at first, but soon the doctor's signed him off for a fortnight and prescribed him some pills. The whole family will be on the tablets at this rate.

Maybe my interest begins to wane a little at this stage. It feels as though there's not much else to get broken. I'm like the child who realises all the plastic air pockets in the sheet of bubble-wrap have been popped. No more noise. Plus he's not so entertaining any more. All that was amusing in him has gone. He's given up telling me how the world should be better organised, how people could make more of themselves, who's just wasting their time. He's more clingy now, and he's morose.

I let it carry on for a few more weeks but I'm more and more reluctant to go round or have him take me out. I can't see the point. Eventually, I stop returning his calls and that sends him into a phoning-frenzy. He must just sit at home and ring all day. There's nothing else doing maybe. I decide to unplug the phone for a while.

Next, he comes round to my flat and buzzes the intercom. I guess that it's him by the drawn-out way he keeps his finger pressed on the button. I'm not going to let him come up, but I answer anyway. *Hello?* And he's off on a rant. I listen to his voice crackling and breaking down the line. He sounds a long way away. I listen for a minute or two but it's boring so I decide to hang up. He buzzes again as soon as he realises that I've put the receiver down, and this time he's shouting. I hang up for a second time and ignore all following buzzes.

When he starts waiting around outside, sitting across the street in his car, I call the police. I tell them I've got a stalker and they come and have words with him, warn him off. He stays away then, but tries a few more times with the phone calls. After ringing in the middle of the night for a couple of nights and not receiving answers (I've switched the ringer to silent), he stops calling.

*

I saw Ian recently; the first time in ages. It'd been about a year. Then the other day, there he was in his car. His wife was with him and the kids were sat in a line on the back seat. He looked older, like he'd lost some more hair. He didn't see me; it was getting dark and his eyes were on the traffic.

So, he's gone back to her, and why not? I'm not bitter. Really, I'm happy for them. They're giving it another shot and good luck to them. They'll need it as well. I wouldn't want that though. I have my own niche to carve, so to speak. And besides, there's plenty more Ians in the world if that's what you're after.

*

One more thing; there are people who'll tell you that they'd always pick the decent road, that in every situation they'd do what's proper, that they'd always be fair and reasonable. That's what they *like* to think and why not believe it if it makes you feel good? They don't *know* though. They don't know what they'd do when push comes to shove. They're just mouthing off about things they don't understand. That's where I'm different. I *know*. I know what the bottom line is. Power is power and everybody wants a slice. *That*'s the bottom line.

# ELIZABETH BAINES
## The Way to Behave

Sisterhood, it's just a wonderful thing.

After all, who do you turn to when your husband's unfaithful with another woman, but the woman herself?

I ring the door bell.

Dark-brown-painted door with frosted panels of early-twentieth-century glass, giving nothing away. A small bay-windowed terrace. Tiny front garden, neat and non-committal with herbs and crazy paving. A single elder casting shadows like a jigsaw puzzle. A suitable home for a woman living alone.

I've no doubt she's single.

I know she's blonde, I found the hair on his jacket, my first proof, talk about pushing me into a cliché.

Of course he denied it, talk about treating a woman with contempt.

The garden slumbers behind me in the autumn sun.

She won't keep me waiting, she knows I'm coming.

I know her voice. This morning, early, she rang the house for the very first time. The sound came through the dawn, through the shrouded rooms and through my dreams, bubbles of it rising from the hall below, the sound of alarm and warning. The sound of guilt and also of plea. I knew straight away, before I'd woken fully, it was the sound I'd been waiting for. A sound being rung for me, not him.

He slept on, foolish man, mobile switched off beside him, hammocked in his complacency and time-honoured male code of divide and rule, a baby glow above his beard.

I got up, made my way down the shadowed stairs, picked up the receiver, the noise ripping, the plug pulled on the secret.

'Hello?'

There was a horrified silence; then, 'Can I speak to Ian?'

She sounded panicked – she must be having some sort of crisis – but there was also curiosity, and abandoned relief.

I didn't need to ask, *Who is this? . . . At this time of the morning?* I side-stepped the stereotype and simply laid down the receiver and went and roused him and watched the game's-up alarm in his opening pale-blue eyes.

I could have killed him, though, for the smoothness with which he changed his expression, sauntered down the stairs with his social-worker's calm, came back and swung his lithe pale legs into his trousers, rolling his eyes about a crisis with a client.

He either thinks I'm a fool or he counts on me wanting to believe him, and who's the bigger fool there, I'd like to know?

He was going down the path when I dialled 1471.

She hadn't withheld her number.

She was at home when I rang her, after I knew he'd be gone to work.

I couldn't help it, I was still so angry, I asked roughly, 'Are you the woman who's trying to grab my husband?'

Another silence filled with horror. Then she said in pain, 'Look. *He* has to be responsible, surely, for his own actions. I'm very fed up with the way he's treating us both, keeping us both in the dark all the time!'

I have to admit I was taken aback. I was silenced a moment. Then, 'Look, can we meet?'

In a rush of relief she cried, 'Oh yes, I think we *should*!'

'Can I come there?'

Alarm. Tentative: 'Well, don't you think we should meet on neutral territory?' And then before I could answer, 'Oh no, of course not, I'm being stupid, that's the language of war, it's not the way to behave! Of course you can come here!'

She moves up behind the frosted panes, the door opens.

She's young, I should have known, her blonde hair in a plait down her back, he always promised he'd never do that, run off with a younger woman, men simply don't know themselves.

She leads me in, looking stricken, compassionate and yet confessional. She invites me to sit in her little front room, yellow with morning sun and sparse with junk-shop furniture.

'You're single?' I ask her.

'Divorced.'

To my shock, I notice children's books on the shelves. 'You've got *children*?'

'Two. Seven and four.'

She pauses. 'Mark, the four-year-old, he's not well, he's asleep upstairs. He had a fever this morning and I couldn't get a doctor. I was very frightened.'

She's looking at me carefully. 'Ian had always told me I must ring if anything like that happened. This time I did.'

I'm silent, taking all this in. At last I say, 'You called his bluff.'

A wry understanding passes between us.

I say bitterly, 'Men are like babies. They want it

all ways.'

She cries in a rush of agreement, 'I *know*!'

'Like to think they're heroes, and all they are are cowards!'

'Oh yes!'

'Relying on us women always to be too frightened to rock the boat!'

'Exactly!'

In spite of all the pain, there's a feeling now of relief, and comradeship even, in the yellow-sun-filled room.

I can't help saying though, 'But don't you think it's immoral, taking advantage, taking someone else's husband?'

She's upset again. 'I don't want to *take* him!'

She sees my look. 'No, no *really*! It has to be up to him! He has to make his own choices. He has to choose, he can't go on keeping us both in misery like this!'

'Keeping his bread buttered both sides.'

'Quite! And honestly,' – she's leaning forward, intent and serious – 'I haven't wanted to deceive you. I've *hated* it! The secrecy, it's so demeaning: for me, and for you! I have begged him to tell you and put us out of our misery. Even if it means I lose him.' She pauses. 'Because, actually, from where I'm standing it's clear he wants to protect his marriage to you at all costs.'

Her creamy face is thrust forward, tragic and brave.

This gives me food for thought, I have to say.

'Yes,' I say. 'He needs to grow up, face up to what he's doing and choose.'

I add, cynical, 'But do we want him now?'

She gives a little sad laugh. We both laugh. The warm sun fills the room. It's almost as if he's written himself out of the equation, it's between me and her now.

'After all,' I say, 'his feet stink.'

'Oh yes, they do!'

'And he's so untidy. He leaves his stuff all over.'

'Oh, I know! He's always leaving plastic bags full of things lying about!'

'And you can't take him anywhere, he's got no social graces.'

'That's very true!'

We laugh again.

Our laughter fades. There's a rueful silence. I break it, 'You don't have a cup of coffee, do you?'

'Oh, of course!' And she rushes off to the kitchen, full of guilt at not having thought of it before, and glad of another way of bridging things between us.

I look around. I realise suddenly why the room is so yellow.

She comes back with the coffee. I say, 'This is my yellow carpet isn't it?'

She's riveted. 'Oh God! He said it was *his*! I mean, even then, I didn't want to accept it, something out of your house . . . But then . . . He said it was up in the attic and not needed, and that *you* hardly knew of its existence . . . And well, it was so cold in here and my kids kept getting ill . . .' She crumples in her chair. 'Oh, I do feel awful.'

'It's okay,' I say quickly. 'Yes, I'd forgotten all about it.' But I can't stop myself saying, 'And that's my blue bowl sitting there on top of your TV.'

She almost dies. 'He said you'd thrown it out! And I really badly didn't want it here, but after all it was his, I mean he's brought so many things he's practically half moved in . . . And if I'd thrown it out too it would be like trashing *you*, trashing his relationship with you, which as I say was the last thing I wanted to do! So I just couldn't touch it and left it there.'

She half collapses. 'It's so *complicated*, this situation he's put us in . . .'

'Don't worry,' I say, 'I had thrown it out.'

She looks unnerved.

I say, 'I must go to the loo.'

'Yes, of course!' She tells me eagerly, 'Straight at the top of the stairs.'

I close the door of the bathroom my husband frequents, where he must have shaved on those mornings after all the nights he's spent away. He's practically half moved in, she said. I open the cabinet, and, sure enough, there are shaving things on its shelves.

I step quietly along the narrow landing past the room with the sleeping child towards the bigger front bedroom. There's the plain double bed where they must lie together, and, sure enough, things of his lying around, clothes belonging to him hanging over a chair . . .

She jumps when I appear in the living-room doorway.

She's been crying, for herself and for me and for the whole ugly mess that we're caught in.

I say, 'I haven't asked you, what do you do?'

She half laughs. 'Exactly. As if we're only defined by our relationship with him! This is what he's done to us!'

She becomes serious. 'I mean, truly: I do love him, but I *could* live without him, because I don't define myself by him. What I define myself by is my work.'

She adds, 'I'm a counsellor, actually.'

I'm taken aback. I have to say I'm stung. The way she says it, she's implying: *Like you*, and it's an apology, for knowing so much more about me than I know about her.

'Hah. You met him through his work then, like

I did.'

She nods. 'Though actually now I'm working with female abuse survivors – up at the Enfield Centre.'

I double-take again. 'I *know* the women who run the Enfield Centre!'

She nods again. 'Yes, I know, I've heard them mention you, but with all the secrecy . . .'

And the look she gives me says: *If it hadn't been for all the secrecy we could have been friends . . . If it hadn't been for the way he divided us . . .*

She says wryly, almost bitterly, 'We have a lot in common, don't we?'

There's silence as we both digest it.

Then: 'So how long has it been going on?'

'Two years.'

For a moment I'm speechless. 'Well, I can't deny then that you do have a claim to him.'

She jumps up, anxious. 'No, no! I keep saying: I'm not making any *claim*! The choice has to be his!'

I contemplate her. 'Well, all I can say is, if it's you he chooses, then good luck to you.'

She's all empathy and sympathy. She's all vindicated sisterhood.

She says, 'And to think that the reason he gave me for not telling you was that you'd take revenge!'

She can't quite see me as I turn on the path, and it's not just the sun in her face, it's the dark glasses I haven't taken off once, merely lifted now and then to poke beneath them and dab at my eyes. She never once saw my eyes. It's the role I came in: he wanted cliché, he could have it – dark-red lips, bitch-painted nails, killer heels. Straight away it unnerved her, and not in the clichéd conventional way: she found it pathetic, and so it put her off guard.

I pan my shades in her direction. She blinks, squints, her blonde hair glistening.

I say, 'I don't intend to be a victim, you know.'

'No, of course not!' she cries with grateful relief.

Sun falls on the elderberry clusters, red veins dripping black blood. I move away beneath the tree, through the tangle of black shadows.

She doesn't know that when I found that hair on his jacket I plucked it off, held it aloft, a gold worm hooked and wriggling on a current of air. He watched speechless, admitting nothing, but understanding everything, as I bore it like a sacrifice to the fire and ceremoniously dropped it in. We both stood and listened to it crackle.


I'm watching from my car in the dark late-afternoon as she leaves the Enfield Centre.

It's her he chose, the woman who could live without him, who said she didn't want to claim him. Once the game was up, he moved out altogether and into hers.

She doesn't notice me. She once knew more about me than I knew about her, but she still won't recognise me. She never really saw me that day, the bitch who stole my things and then snatched away my husband, who pulls his lithe pale limbs around her, whose brats he left my bed to go to, trashing his past as a parent with me. Unaware, she gets into her car, the woman who did all this and then thought she could get treated like my sister, pious mealy-mouthed cow.

I want to kill her. I start up quickly and bear down as she slows at the entrance. I see my lights flash like dragon's eyes in her mirror, I see her head jerk up in alarm. As she accelerates I'm right on her tail.

She can't lose me. I keep my foot down, we're

doing fifty, she's guessed it's me, but I'm a roaring impersonal dragon behind her, I can feel her terror through all that hot metal.

At last I slow, I won't kill myself too. I let her go for now, the woman who says she'd rather be defined by her work.

I'm watching again the day she's told in no uncertain terms that her services are no longer welcome at the centre. She comes down the steps, her face a white smudge of shock.

I knew it wouldn't play well with my women contacts at the centre. I knew that when I pointed out to them that for two whole years she'd colluded with a man's abuse of another woman, they'd feel that it compromised her position as a counsellor to women abused by men. I knew they'd feel she could no longer be trusted, especially when I drew their attention to the fact that for all that time she'd carefully deceived them too. And as they said then themselves (veterans as they are of the old Sisterhood days): in view of my recent state, and the crucial time that I've consequently lost with my own female clients, she's damaged the cause and hampered a lot of other women's lives . . .

She crosses the car park like a sleepwalker doomed.

He's moving back home.

I knew exactly how she'd feel. I knew she'd consider that ultimately it wasn't I but he who had ruined her career. That if he hadn't behaved in the way that he did, then I'd never have been driven to take revenge.

Sisterhood, eh?

# About the Authors

**Sherry Ashworth** has written a number of novels for both adults and teenagers, including *A Matter of Fat*, which was first published by Crocus, *The Dream Travellers, Paralysed* and most recently *Close Up*. Her young adult novel *Blinded by the Light* won the North East Book Award. She lives in Manchester with her husband, two daughters – and two cats.

**Elizabeth Baines** is the author of numerous published short stories and the novels *Body Cuts* and the critically acclaimed *The Birth Machine*. She is also an award-winning playwright for radio and stage, and in July 2005 performed her own monologue, *Drinks with Natalie*, for the Manchester 24:7 Theatre Festival.

**Maya Chowdhry** grew up in Scotland; is a poet, playwright and inTer-aCt-ive artist. Her award-winning work has been published and performed nationally and internationally. In 1992 she won the Cardiff International Poetry Competition. She believes in writing from 'under the skin' and has worked with numerous communities facilitating their voices. She was a member of the editorial collective of *Feminist Arts News* and co-edited *Acts of Passion: Sexuality, Gender and Performance*. Maya was writer-on-attachment at the National Theatre Studio in 2002 and is working on a collection of digital poetry, *destinyNation*, for which she received an Arts Council literature award.

**Suzanne Elvidge** is based in Yorkshire and is the head of publishing for a medical consulting company. She has been writing since she could clutch a crayon.

She writes short stories, poetry and articles, and runs occasional writing workshops, and has had stories and poems for adults and children published in anthologies and magazines. She is on the Yorkshire Art Circus writer development programme and keeps threatening to write a novel. More likely to be found in a cycling helmet than a hat and pearls, Suzanne loves reading, swimming, gardening, listening to jazz and harassing her cats Satchmo and Dizzie.

**Michelle Green** is a Manchester-based writer who regularly dishes up her social soul rants and rhymes at live events across the UK. Her poems and short stories have appeared in a variety of anthologies, publications and radio shows, including 2002's *City Secrets* anthology of short stories. Following years of home-based 'zine production, her first collection of poems will be published by Crocus in 2006.

**Sophie Hannah** is a best-selling poet, a novelist and a regular performer of her own work. Her first collection of short stories, *We All Say What We Want*, will be published by Sort Of Books in 2007. Her psychological suspense story, *The Octopus Nest* won first prize in the 2005 Daphne du Maurier Festival Short Story Competition, and in April 2006, Hodder published her first crime novel, *Little Face*. Sophie's latest poetry collection, *First of the Last Chances*, was chosen for the Poetry Society's Next Generation promotion, recognising her as one of the best poets to emerge in the last ten years. She lives in Bingley, West Yorkshire.

**Misha Herwin** has been writing from the moment she could hold a pen. At twelve her first play featured a witch queen and was staged in a Victorian theatre made from a cardboard box. Since then she has had plays published by Carel Press and others commissioned by Stagefright Theatre Company. While living in Jamaica, she worked in down town Kingston and wrote a novel about expat life. She is currently working as a supply teacher, writing in the evenings and weekends. Her ambition is to write full time and in this she has fantastic support from her husband, family and writing group.

**Liz Kirby** is a poet, with a long history of publishing; most recently in *Famous Reporter* (Australia), *dANDdelion* (Canada), on the website of Wild Honey Press (www.wildhoneypress.com) and on the stones of the quarries above Rawtenstall in the Rossendale Valley. At present she is absorbed in the process of redrafting her first novel which is set in the Peak District of the eighth century. She is a member of the Thaumaturgist Movement – a gathering of artists, musicians and writers/performers dedicated to manifesting magic, miracles and wonders. *Lambswool* could be seen as the first Thaumaturgist short story!

**Bren Lucas** was born and brought up in Huddersfield, West Yorkshire, and worked in the textile mills before marrying and starting a family. Married to Steve, she has two grown-up children and recently started writing and painting now that she has a little time for herself. *Reader, I Mullered Him* is her first published story.

**Rosie Lugosi** has an eclectic writing and performance history, ranging from singing in eighties goth band The March Violets, to her current incarnation as Rosie Lugosi the Vampire Queen, electrifying performer-poet, compère and singer. As well as three solo collections of poetry (*Hell and Eden, Coming Out at Night* and *Creatures of the Night*), her award-winning short stories, poems and essays have been widely anthologised. *Mapping the Interior*, her first novel, is currently with an agent. She has won both the Erotic Oscar for Performance Artist of the Year and the Diva Award for Solo Performer. For more information visit her website: www.rosielugosi.co.uk

**Char March** is an award-winning poet and playwright. Her credits include: three collections of poetry, five BBC Radio 4 plays and seven stage plays. Her poetry and short fiction have been published widely in literary magazines and anthologies. Char is currently working on her first novel and her sixth radio play. She grew up in Scotland and now divides her time between the Highlands and Yorkshire.

**Susannah Marshall** wrote this story having commuted to Manchester from Leeds on a daily basis for two years. She is currently completing a degree in graphic design, and lives in Leeds with her wonderful partner, Claudia, and their three children and two dogs. She has never driven a truck.

**Brighid Rose** was born in 1969. After graduating from a fine art degree in 1992, Brighid worked for several years in an art studio in Nottingham, exhibiting her work around the East Midlands. She subsequently moved to live near the Findhorn Community in northern Scotland where her focus turned more towards writing and in 2002 she undertook a Creative Writing MA at Lancaster University. Since graduating, Brighid has worked on completing her first novel, a 'dystopian fairy-tale', *A Bad Transaction in the City of Lists*. She now produces both art and written work.

Brighid lives on a narrowboat on a West Yorkshire canal.

**Chris Scholes** was born in Lancashire and educated in Yorkshire. Her short stories have been broadcast on television and radio, and published in magazines and several anthologies. She has formerly been short-listed for the Asham Prize and has an MA in Writing. Chris lives in splendid isolation on the beautiful Saddleworth Moors. She loves olives, wine, figs and sunny days.

**Mary Sharratt** is an American writer currently living in a dark satanic mill town in East Lancashire. Winner of the 2005 WILLA Literary Award for Contemporary Fiction, she is the author of the novels *Summit Avenue*, *The Real Minerva* and *The Vanishing Point*. Her short fiction has been published widely in journals and anthologies, including *The Year's Best Fantasy and Horror* and *Twin Cities Noir*. Her Bitch Lit story *Family Man* is part of a new novel-in-progress, *The Art of Memory*. Mary teaches writing and is a reviews editor for the Historical Novel Society. Visit her website: www.marysharratt.com

**Cath Staincliffe** writes the acclaimed Sal Kilkenny mysteries. *Looking for Trouble* won the Crocus Novel Competition and launched private eye Sal, a single parent struggling to juggle work and home, onto Manchester's mean streets. It was short-listed for the Crime Writers Association best first novel award and serialised on Radio 4, *Woman's Hour*. The sixth and latest mystery is *Bitter Blue*. Cath is also a scriptwriter, creator of ITV's hit police series, *Blue Murder*, starring Caroline Quentin. She is a founder member of Murder Squad, a collective of crime writers who promote their work through readings, workshops and events.

**Dr Jo Stanley** is a writer and historian specialising in creative lifestory work with socially excluded groups. Her day job is artist in residence at a hospice. However, this story is entirely fictional. In her night work she is an internationally recognised expert on gender in maritime history. Her books include *Hello Sailor: the Hidden History of Gay Life at Sea*; *Writing Out your Life: a Guide to Writing Creative Autobiography*; and *Bold in her Breeches: Women Pirates Across the Ages*. She lives in Yorkshire where she roams the moors, and wishes she had time to write more fiction.

**Lynne Taylor** writes because she has to. It's a compulsion. And therapeutic: it helps her to get in touch with herself; make sense of life. Her fundamental fascination is what makes people tick and how they affect one another. Then to imagine the consequences. Writing for her is like acting on paper. She lives the character. And finds this addictively liberating. She has no idea what inspired this story. And she's not consulting Freud. TS Eliot said that a true writer does not write about the experiences he's had, but about the experiences he's about to have. Gulp.

**Louise Wilford**, who returned to her birthplace in South Yorkshire five years ago having spent more than a decade 'down south', teaches English, but makes life worth living by writing in her spare time. She has written many short stories and poems, and has won several creative writing prizes in recent years. She has co-written two sitcom scripts, and has written articles for *Ink Pellet* magazine and *The Times Educational*

*Supplement.* She is currently working on a children's fantasy novel and a stage-play, and attempting to study for a Master's in Literature.